"I thought I might announce my impending marriage."

Her eyebrows shot up. "Marriage? You aren't getting married."

"No. But don't you think it would make a nice headline?"

She let out a completely undignified involuntary snort. "No one would believe it."

"And why is that?"

"Marriage requires monogamy," she said.

"I don't cheat on women. If I'm attracted to someone else, I end the relationship I'm in. I see no point in pretending to want one woman if I want another."

"You seem to change the woman you want with alarming frequency."

"And that's why it would be such a big story if I were preparing to get married."

"Okay, yeah, I'll give you that. But where are we going to find a woman who won't want to marry you for real? One who will keep her mouth shut about the arrangement?"

She looked back at Gage. His blue eyes were trained on her, a slow smile spreading over his handsome face.

"Lily. I want you to marry me."

Maisey Yates

MARRIAGE MADE ON PAPER

21st CENTURY BOSSES

TORONTO NEW YORK LONDON
AMSTERDAM PARIS SYDNEY HAMBURG
STOCKHOLM ATHENS TOKYO MILAN MADRID
PRAGUE WARSAW BUDAPEST AUCKLAND

Recycling programs
for this product may
not exist in your area.

ISBN-13: 978-0-373-13016-0

MARRIAGE MADE ON PAPER

First North American Publication 2011

www.Harlequin.com

Printed in U.S.A.

MARRIAGE MADE
ON PAPER

CHAPTER ONE

LILY FORD wasn't thrilled to see Gage Forrester standing in her office, leaning over her desk, his large masculine hands clasping the edge, his scent teasing her, making her heart beat at an accelerated pace. *She* wasn't thrilled to see Gage, the man who had turned her down, but her body seemed to be on a different wavelength.

"I heard that Jeff Campbell hired your company," he said, leaning in a little more, his shoulder muscles rolling forward. He certainly didn't spend all of his time behind a desk in a corporate office. A physique like that didn't happen by accident. She knew that from personal experience.

It took her four evenings a week in the gym to combat the effects of her mostly sedentary job. But it was important. Image counted for a lot, and it was her job to keep the images of her clients sparkling clean in the public eye. She felt that if her own image wasn't up to par she would lose her credibility.

"You heard correctly," she said, leaning back in her chair, trying to put some distance between them. Trying to feel as if she had some measure of control. It was her office, darn it. He had no call coming in here and trying to assume authority.

But then, men like Gage operated that way. They came, they saw, they conquered the female.

Not this female.

"So, are you here to offer me congratulations?" she asked sweetly.

"No, I'm here to offer you a contract."

That successfully shocked her into silence, which was a rare thing. "You rejected my offer to represent your company, Mr. Forrester."

"And now I'm extending you an offer."

She pursed her lips. "Does this have anything to do with the fact that Jeff Campbell is your biggest competitor?"

"I don't consider him a competitor." Gage smiled, but in his eyes she could see the glint of steel, the hardness that made him a legend in his industry. You didn't reach greatness by being soft. She knew it, she respected it. But she didn't necessarily care for Gage, or his business practices. Generally speaking, she thought that he was somewhat morally bankrupt. But an account with Forrestation Inc. would be a huge boon for her company. The biggest account she'd ever had.

"Like it or not, he is your competitor. And he's quite good at what he does. He doesn't leave half the mess for me to clean up that you would."

"Which is why he isn't really my competition. He's too politically correct, too concerned with his public image."

"It wouldn't hurt you to be more concerned with it. The endless stream of actresses and supermodels on your arm doesn't exactly give off an aura of stability. Plus you've had a series of very unpopular builds lately."

"Is this a free consultation?"

"No. I'm charging you by the half hour."

"If I remember correctly your services aren't cheap."

"They aren't. If you want cheap, you have to suffer incompetence."

He sat down on the edge of her desk and effectively threw half of her office supplies out of alignment. Annoyance coursed through her, along with the desire to reach out and straighten her stapler, which was nearly as strong as the need she suddenly felt to touch his thigh, so close to her hand now, and find out if it was as hard and muscular as it looked.

She grimaced at her own line of thinking, her train of thought irritating and confusing her. She didn't indulge in fantasies about men, she just didn't.

"That's one thing I liked about you when I interviewed you, Lily. You're confident in your skills."

"What was it you didn't like about me, Mr. Forrester? Because as you and I both know, you hired Synergy to represent your company, not me."

"I make it a practice not to hire women under a certain age. Particularly if they're attractive."

She felt her mouth fall open in shock, and she knew she looked like some sort of gasping guppy, but there was nothing she could do combat it. "That's sexist."

"Maybe. But I haven't had to deal with unwanted affections from my male personal assistant, unlike my previous PA, who fell hopelessly in love with me."

"Maybe you were imagining things. Or maybe you encouraged her." Privately, she had to admit that Gage was an attractive man, but that didn't mean that every woman under a certain age was immediately going to fall in love at first sight with him. Yet he probably believed it. Power did that to people, men especially. They started thinking of everyone as their property, like they were entitled to the slavish devotion of everyone around them.

Some men didn't even need wealth. They just needed someone weaker than they were.

She shook off the memories that were creeping in.

"I wasn't imagining it, trust me. And I never encouraged her," Gage said. "I was never interested in her. Business is business, sex is sex."

"Never the twain shall meet?"

"Exactly. To compound the matter, when I fired her she made a huge scene."

"Why did you fire her?"

One dark eyebrow shot up. "I came into the office one morning to find her perched naked on my desk in a pose that would make a centerfold blush."

Lily's mouth dropped open. "Are you serious?"

"Unfortunately, yes. But since then, I haven't hired women to work closely with me, and since then, I haven't had any other issues." He regarded her closely. "You aren't engaged or expecting a baby anytime soon, are you?"

She almost laughed. "No worries there, Mr. Forrester. I have no plans for wedding or baby in the near, or distant, future. My career is my focus."

"I've heard that said by more than one woman, more than once. But then the woman meets a man who makes her hear wedding bells, and I end up having wasted my time training someone who never intended to stay on with the company."

"If I ever hear wedding bells, Mr. Forrester, you have my guarantee that I will run in the opposite direction."

"Good."

"I still think you're sexist. Assuming that just because a woman is a…a woman…she's going to fall madly in love with you the moment she looks into your eyes, or that the moment she gets a job she's going to run off and get married and abandon everything she's worked for."

"I'm not sexist. It's called covering your bases. I don't make the same mistake twice. But I've seen the press releases you've prepared for Campbell. I've also watched his stocks go up."

"Yours have been going up, too," she added.

"That may be, but his were on their way down. The only thing that's changed is his hiring you."

She held a hand out, pretending to examine her merlot-colored nails, hoping he didn't notice the slight tremor in her fingers. "So, now you want me to go back on my contract with Mr. Campbell? It would have to be a pretty sweet offer, Mr. Forrester."

"It is." He named a figure that made her heart slam into her ribs.

She'd been working so hard, struggling to keep things going with her small public relations firm for so long the thought of all that money made her feel light-headed.

And money was only part of it. There was the notoriety, good and bad, that would come from working for Forrestation. Gage had a reputation as being a bit of a rogue, which was both appealing and frightening to investors. He took risks, sometimes at the expense of popularity, and they paid off.

Some of his larger building projects had been unpopular with a vocal minority, and while the hotel properties had been resounding successes once completed, he'd had protestors lining the streets in front of his San

Diego office building on more than one occasion. A lot of the protests were simply against any new building being built, but some of the issues had seemed understandable to Lily.

As controversial as Gage might be, he was a billionaire for a reason. And even if, sometimes, she had sympathized with the protesters, she couldn't argue with the numbers.

"Say I was interested," she said, feigning a lot more absorption in her manicure than she felt. "There's an early termination fee on my contract with Mr. Campbell."

"I'll cover it."

She blinked. "And I need an expense account."

He leaned in slightly, his scent—she was noticing it again for the second time in ten minutes—making her heart beat faster. "Done, as long as you don't consider manicures a business expense." He reached out and took her hand in his for a moment.

His hands were rough. Rougher than she imagined a man with a desk job's hands would be. It was just the right amount, though. Not too rough that having him touch her was uncomfortable. Although his skin was hot, and it made a rash of heat flare through her body, raising her core temperature at a rate that didn't seem physically possible.

She tugged her hand back, trying to seem as though his casual touch hadn't just flustered her like that. Nothing flustered her. Ever. She didn't *do* flustered. Especially not during business hours.

She cleared her throat. "I don't. Although I consider image to be an extremely important part of my job. I always present myself in a professional, polished manner. Your presentation and my presentation matter to each other. Our success is linked, which makes our business relationship very important."

"Is that your standard speech?"

She felt her cheeks heat slightly. "Yes."

"I can tell. It's very well-rehearsed. And I think I heard it during your interview."

She tightened her lips, trying to hold her temper in check. Something about Gage made her feel very shaky and almost…unpredictable. He brought her emotions very close to the surface. Emotions she was usually very good at holding down.

"Well, rehearsed or not," she said, eyes narrowed, "it's true. The better I look, the better I make you look, the more money you make. And the better you behave, the better you follow my advice, the more money you make, the more success I'll have."

"So, is this lecture your form of consent?"

"Yes," she said, not missing a beat.

"I want you to work with me personally. I don't want anyone else on your team involved with my account. It has to be you."

"I wouldn't have it any other way."

"The building project in Thailand is already controversial, which has my shareholders clutching their wallets in terror."

"And what about the Thailand project is controversial?"

"The fear that by building more resorts we're distorting local culture. That such a Westernized focus doesn't show people the real Thailand. That we're giving tourists a theme park rather than reality."

"And are you?"

He shrugged. "Does it matter to you?"

"I don't have to like you, Mr. Forrester, I just have to make sure everyone else does."

"So, even if you did have a personal problem with the project?"

"Like the wedding bells, not an issue. This is business. My business is presenting your best to the public and to your shareholders."

"I need to get the details hammered out as quickly as possible." He leaned over and picked his briefcase up from the floor, opened it and pulled out a thick stack of papers. "This is the contract. If you need anything changed, let me know and we'll discuss it. And you need to terminate your dealings with Jeff Campbell. One thing I require is that your firm no longer represent him in any capacity. Conflict of interest."

"Of course."

He looked at her, and reached across her desk, picking up her cell phone and holding it out to her.

"What? You want me to call now?"

"Time is money, or so I've heard."

She snatched the phone from his hand and dialed Jeff's number, her palms slick with sweat. She hated that he had the ability to make her lose her cool. It didn't help that Jeff Campbell had definitely been giving her the "let's make this business into pleasure" vibe. Which made terminating the contract sting just a little bit less, as the last thing she wanted to deal with was working with a man with sex on his brain.

The phone rang once before Jeff answered. "Hi, it's Lily."

Gage raised his eyebrows but didn't comment.

"I know." Jeff sounded far too pleased about it for her peace of mind, his tone of voice almost intimate. It made her skin crawl.

"I'm really sorry to have to tell you this, but I've been offered a better contract and I feel I can't afford to turn it down."

She listened while Jeff expressed his disappointment, in a very nice fashion, considering she was breaking a contract they'd drawn up a week ago. He was probably still hoping to get a date. Which was confirmed when he asked if they could meet over dinner to discuss it further.

"Sorry. I'm going to be really busy with…work. Because of the contract. The new one." Gage's blue eyes were locked on her and it was making her nervous, which she hated. Men never upset her personal balance. She never let them close enough to do that.

"There's a monetary penalty for terminating the contract," Jeff said, his voice icy now.

"I know. I was there when the addition was made and I read the contract thoroughly before I signed it." She looked at Gage, trying to judge his reaction. "But this is a business move that I feel I have to make. It's the best thing for my company."

"So ethics, fulfilling your commitments, aren't as important as money?"

Ouch. She took a breath. "It's business, Jeff. In my position you would do the same. Business is business," she said, unconsciously echoing Gage's earlier statement.

"You certainly never treated it like it was only a business arrangement." The inference and the venom in his tone shocked her. Though she knew it shouldn't. Men seemed to think a polite greeting meant she wanted to hop into bed with them. And that was their problem, not hers.

"Sorry to have given you the wrong impression," she

bit out, conscious of Gage's close study of her. "But as far as I'm concerned, yes, it was only a business arrangement. And now, it's a defunct business arrangement."

Gage took the phone from her hand, his expression far too satisfied for her liking. "Just wanted to affirm that Lily is working for me now."

And now Lily felt like a treat being fought over by two dogs, and it was not pretty. She didn't like that she was in the middle of some kind of alpha war. And the feeling was only magnified by the fact that Jeff had, apparently, assumed she was interested in him as more than just a source of income.

She could hear the tone, not the words, to Jeff's curt reply before Gage snapped her phone shut and set it back on the desk.

She stood up and rounded the desk, reckless anger coursing through her. "This is my office, Mr. Forrester. I might be working for you but I expect you to remember that."

"You're working for me, Ms. Ford, that's the bottom line, whether we're in your office or mine." His blue eyes held that steel that made him so successful.

On the outside he might seem like the kind of man who didn't take life seriously. The endless succession of models and actresses on his arms saw that he featured in the tabloids regularly, and he'd garnered a reputation as a playboy. But she knew that he hadn't reached the level of success he had without an edge of ruthlessness. He didn't often put it on show, but then, he wouldn't have to. The man radiated power. And beneath that she sensed that he had the soul of a predator. The fact that he was in her office now was proof of that.

At one time that would have intimidated her. *He* would have intimidated her. But not anymore. She was an up-and-coming player in the business world, and she wasn't going to reach her destination by backing down.

But she hadn't gotten where she was by being stupid, either, and even if she was angry beyond reason that Gage was usurping her authority in her own office, she wasn't about to spar with her brand-new boss.

"I apologize," she said, lowering the register of her voice, trying to project a calmer demeanor than she currently felt capable of projecting. "But I have to confess I'm a little bit controlling and I can be very territorial."

Gage tried to ignore the tightening in his gut. The woman practically purred when she spoke. And when she stood from her desk, she sauntered around to the other side, her walk as slinky and liquid as a cat's, her curves enough to remind him why it was so good to be a man.

She was stunning, not like the women he usually dated with their breezy West Coast manner, and their fake-and-bake tans. She was more like a museum display. Refined, elegant and partitioned off with thick velvet rope. She had Do Not Touch signs all over her, and yet, like a museum display, that made her all the more tempting.

She tilted her head and put one perfectly manicured hand on her shapely hip. Her skirt-and-jacket combo was expertly tailored to skim her curves, revealing her figure, but not in an obvious way. Her dark brown hair was twisted into a neat bun and her pale, flawless skin, rare in the sun-obsessed state of California, had just the right amount of makeup to look a bit more perfect than nature allowed.

"What are your terms?" she asked.

"My terms?"

"What do you expect from me so that I may be worthy of the somewhat exorbitant sum you're offering me?"

She had attitude, but that was a good thing. She would be dealing with the media on his behalf, and in order to do that, she was going to need a backbone of steel. She seemed eager to prove that it was firmly in place.

"If you really think the sum is exorbitant I could always offer you less."

"I could never turn down your generosity, it would be rude."

He chuckled. "Well, in the interest of good manners, by all means, accept it. As for the rest, I expect you to be on call twenty-four hours a day, seven days a week. I have projects happening all over the world in several different time zones, that means it's always business hours. That means if something happens and I need my PR specialist, you have to be available. I can't afford for you be off on a hot date."

"Your chauvinistic nature is showing again, but I assure you that nothing takes priority over my job. Not even hot dates." She quirked a dark eyebrow, her brown eyes glittering. She liked this, challenging him, he could tell. And he took it as a good sign. His last public relations specialist had cracked under the pressure in less than a year. It was a hard business, even harder in his industry and with his level of visibility in the media. The fact that Lily seemed to enjoy a little bit of friction was a good sign.

"In that case why don't you get down to the business of signing your life away to me?" he said.

A faint smile curved her berry-painted lips and she

turned to face her desk, grabbed a pen out of the holder and bent over slightly so that she could sign the contract. It was a pose she had to know was provocative. Her fitted pencil skirt cupped the round curve of her butt so snugly he couldn't help but admire the flawless shape. And she had to know that. Women always knew. No wonder Jeff Campbell had assumed she'd been making a play for him. Deluded idiot. Lily wasn't making an offer, she was out to intimidate. And on most men, he could see how it might work. But not on him.

She straightened and turned, her jaw set, her expression one of satisfied determination. She extended her hand and he took it. She shook it firmly, her dark eyes shining with triumph.

"I look forward to doing business with you, Mr. Forrester."

He laughed. "You say that now, Ms. Ford, but you haven't started the job yet."

CHAPTER TWO

THE fact that the very first thing she felt when Gage's deep, masculine voice pulled her out of the deep sleep she'd been in was a shiver of excitement, and not a pang of annoyance, was disturbing on a lot of levels, all of which she was too tired to analyze in that moment.

"It's one in the morning, Gage." Lily blinked against the blinding light radiating from the screen of her smartphone. After four months in his employ, she should know better than to be surprised by a midnight phone call.

"It's nine a.m. in England."

"And we have a crisis on our hands?" She rolled over and brushed her hair out of her face, the cool sheets from the side of the bed that had been unoccupied chilling her slightly.

"The sky isn't falling, if that's what you mean, but we have protesters lining the streets at our newest building site and I need a press release that will help cool things down."

"Now?"

"Preferably before the mob tears down the foundation of our new hotel," he bit out.

Lily sat up and swung her legs over the side of the bed, pushing the button for speakerphone and bringing up the specs of the project up on the screen. "What's the issue?"

"Environmental impact."

She studied the report. "It's a green build. Recycled materials are being used for as much of the hotel as possible, anything that isn't is being purchased locally and it's helping to stimulate local economy."

"Good. Put all of that in a press release and get it sent."

"Just a second. I was in bed. Asleep. Like a normal person," she said, sleep depravation making her grumpy.

She stood and made her way to her desk, which she had moved a mere foot away from her bed just for such occasions. Her laptop was still fired up, so she sat down, dashed off all of the necessary info and emailed it to Gage. "How's that?"

"Good," he responded a few moments later. "What do you suggest? Written or verbal?"

"Both. Call down there and see if you can speak to someone on the phone. I'll contact the local news station. Then we'll work on getting it into online editions of the papers today and print for tomorrow. That ought to defuse things, as much as possible anyway. They still might not be happy about the build in general, but if you show that you're conscientious it should go a long way in smoothing things over, at least with the general public, which is really the best you can hope for."

"You really are good," he said, that voice sending a little frisson of...something...through her again. She'd thought she would get used to him in the months since he'd walked into her office and hired her. In a lot of ways she had, but he still had the ability to throw her off balance if she wasn't prepared for him.

"I'm the best, Gage," she said sharply, "don't forget it."

"How can I? You never let me."

"I hope you mean in deed rather than word," she said archly.

"Take your pick."

"All right. I'm going to call some televisions stations and then I'm going back to bed."

"Fine, but I need you in the office by five."

She bit back a groan. "Of course." It was likely he was already at the office. Between work and dalliances with supermodels she wasn't sure if Gage Forrester ever slept.

She hung up the phone and proceeded to make her phone calls before falling back into bed. She could get two good hours before she had to be in the office.

And why did Gage's voice seem to be echoing in her mind while she tried to drift off?

She walked into Gage's office at 4:59 a.m. with two industrial-sized cups of coffee. "Thought you might need a hit," she said, setting the cup down in front of him.

He looked up from his computer screen. Annoyingly, despite the five-o'clock shadow he was sporting he looked fresh and well-rested, while she knew she had puffy eyes that were just barely made to look normal by gobs of under-eye cream.

"I definitely need a hit," he said, picking up the cup and bringing it to his lips. She couldn't help but watch him, the way his lips moved to cover the opening of the lid, the slight view of his tongue. His mouth fascinated her. Like the effect his voice seemed to have on her, she was certain she didn't want to know why his mouth fascinated her.

Well, she knew why. It was the same reason an endless stream of beautiful women were constantly on his arm. The same reason she did as much talking to the press about his personal life as she did about his professional life. Gage Forrester was one sexy man. Even she could admit that.

In theory, she liked sexy men, at least from a distance. When said sexy man was her boss, it made life a bit more complicated. It didn't really matter, though. Business was business and she had no intention of crossing any lines with him. She wasn't his type anyway. He liked party girls. The shallower, and the shorter the skirt, the better. And he definitely wasn't her type. Of course, she wasn't entirely certain what her type was as far as practical application went. Judging by her recent string of failed dates she didn't really have a type.

"How many shots?" he asked, lowering the cup.

"Quad," she answered, trying to bring her mind back into the present and away, far, far away, from his lips.

"Good. It's going to be a long day."

She sat down in the chair by his desk, pulled her notebook out of her briefcase and sat poised with a pen in her hand.

"Why do you do that?" he asked.

"Do what?"

"Take physical notes on paper. You have a million little gadgets for that kind of thing. I know because most of them were purchased with your expense account."

"This helps me commit it to memory. I always log it electronically later."

A small smile curved his lips, lips she was staring at again. She looked down at her notebook.

"The England site, how do you feel about the damage control that's been done there?"

"Great," she said. "You have a satellite interview scheduled with one of the news outlets very late tonight. Also, the written release is set to run in major newspapers tomorrow, and you spoke to the organizer of the protests personally, right?"

"Yes. Nice woman. Didn't like me very much. I think she called me a...capitalist pig."

She looked up and her heart jumped a bit. She looked back down at the lined paper of her notebook. "You kind of are."

"A rich one."

"Touché."

"I was able to explain to her the process by which we're building the hotel. I also explained, very nicely, how it would help the economy, and that, in addition to the construction workers who have work now, it would provide at least a hundred permanent positions. And the fact that it's being built on the site of what was essentially a crumbling wreck of an old manor, and not on any farmland, went over well."

"All very good," Lily said, scribbling on her notebook before reaching over to grab her coffee cup off of Gage's desk and taking a sip.

In the beginning it had seemed strange, coming in early when no one else was in the building, sitting in Gage's luxurious office, watching the sunrise, glinting off the bay, and the hundreds of boats moored in the San Diego harbor. It had almost seemed...intimate in some ways. Half the time he hadn't shaved yet when she arrived, and he would go into his private bathroom that adjoined his office and take care of it before the other staff arrived, but he didn't bother for her.

"Anything else on the agenda?" she asked.

"I need a date for an event tomorrow. Fundraiser. Art gala."

"And you've misplaced your little black book?"

"No, it's in a safe somewhere so that no one can ever get their hands on it and use it for evil."

"*You* use it for evil," she said.

"On occasion. But the real issue is that none of my black book entries are suitable."

"Well that sounds like an issue of taste to me," she said. It bothered her sometimes—okay, all the time—that a man with his drive to succeed dated women who were such bubbleheads. But then, she didn't imagine he was interested in the contents of their minds.

"No, it's an issue of venue. I want you to go with me."

"What?"

"But you need something else to wear."

She narrowed her eyes. "What?"

"You're intelligent. You know how to make conversation."

"So do most women. You just tend to date women who can't talk and walk at the same time without injuring themselves."

"I didn't know you had an opinion on my choice of companion."

She gritted her teeth. "Doesn't matter, what matters is that I shield the public from the full horror of it. And what's wrong with the way I dress?"

She spent an obscene amount of money buying good quality clothing and having it tailored. She always, always, looked polished and ready for a press conference. Always. It was essential to her job and she took it very seriously.

"Nothing. If you have a business meeting. But you look more like a politician's wife than a woman I would take to a fundraiser."

"Politicians' wives go to fundraisers."

"But I'm not a politician."

"And I'm not for hire."

His dark brows locked together. "No. You're not, because I already hired you. You work for me, and if I need you I expect you to make yourself available. You signed a contract agreeing to it."

"To be your PR specialist at all hours, which is quite enough, thank you very much, not to hang on your arm at art galas."

"This is PR. I could skip the fundraiser and look like a capitalist pig with no conscience, or I could go with Shan Carter. She gave me her number the other night."

An image of the spoiled blonde heiress in her thigh-high boots and cling-wrap dress flashed before Lily's eyes.

"You can't do that," she said, all of her PR training recoiling in horror at the thought.

"I know. I didn't even need you to tell me."

"Fine. I'll go. But you're not picking my dress."

His icy gaze swept her up and down. "*You're* not."

"Why not? You've never seen me in date clothes. You don't know what my date clothes look like." She didn't own date clothes, but he didn't have to know that. She had confidence in her taste in clothes. She knew what she looked good in and she really didn't need some wafer-thin personal shopper to try and tell her what she already knew.

"All right, but no tweed."

"I don't wear tweed. Well, I have a jacket that's

tweed, but it's chic. Lycra isn't the official fabric of fashion, you know. Though I know you couldn't prove it by your dates."

He shrugged in that casual manner of his, that shrug that seemed especially designed to provoke her. "I like to have fun. I work hard. My obligations are met. I see no issue with conducting my personal life in the way I see fit."

He had a point, as much as she hated to admit it. Although she couldn't imagine why any woman in her right mind would date him. Well, that was a lie, it was obvious visually why a woman would want to date him. He was tall, broad-shouldered and perfectly built. But on a personal level, while he was smart and fun to banter with, he was also totally uncompromising when it came down to it, and she knew she could never deal with a man like that. She'd seen the kind of toll a man like that could take on a woman's life. And she'd vowed she wouldn't become like that. She wasn't letting anyone have control over her life.

Although, obviously Gage had some modicum of control over her life since he was her boss, but that was different. When a woman gave a man her body he owned a piece of her. She thought the whole thing was just entirely too unsettling. And no matter how gorgeous Gage was, it wasn't enough to erase the memories that she carried with her. Warnings. Her mother's mistakes had to count for something, otherwise they really would be a complete tragedy, and as contentious as her relationship with her mother was, she didn't want that.

"If you expect me to buy new clothes you have to give me time to shop."

"You can have the afternoon off."

She shook her head, her tight bun staying firmly in place. "Morning and afternoon. I need sleep."

"Morning to lunch hour," he countered.

"Deal."

"No black. No beige."

"It's an art gala, most of the women will be in black."

"I know, and that's exactly why I want you to wear something else."

She frowned. "I'm not in the habit of allowing men to dictate what I wear. I can choose for myself."

He stood from his desk, and she was distracted, as she always was when he surprised her like that, by the superb shape of his body. Narrow waist, broad chest. And she knew, though she was ashamed to admit it, that he also had the best butt she'd ever seen. Although she hadn't taken notice of very many men in that way before, so she didn't have much to compare to.

He raised an eyebrow. "So if your lover had a preference for lingerie you wouldn't consider that, either?"

She bit the inside of her cheek and tried to will herself not to blush. She never let men rattle her. She'd been on the receiving end of pick-up lines from cheesy to crude since she began to develop at the age of thirteen, and then, after she'd moved and started her new life, men had naturally assumed she was ready to bed-hop her way to the top of the corporate ladder. As a result, she'd assumed she'd lost the ability to blush a long time ago. Apparently not. She felt her face get hot.

She'd never worried about her lack of sexual experience. It was a choice she'd made. In the environment she'd been raised in it had been a fight to hold on to any sort of innocence, physical or psychological, and she'd been determined that no one would take it from her.

But in that moment she knew she would rather walk across broken glass than admit that no man had ever had cause to have an opinion about her lingerie.

"I have impeccable taste," she said instead, lifting her chin, trying to keep her expression smooth. Cool. Not completely flustered. "No one has ever had reason to complain." She picked her briefcase up from the floor and stood. "And neither will you." She turned on her heel and stalked out of the office, trying to ignore the thundering of her heart.

CHAPTER THREE

GAGE had never seen Lily look less than perfect. She always looked beautiful, even when she rushed into the office at two in the morning to handle some sort of media crisis. But in a dark navy blue gown with ruffled sleeves, a demure neckline and a back that dipped so low it ought to be illegal, she was stunning.

Her hair was pinned to the side so that her curls cascaded over one shoulder, and didn't cover any of the skin that was on display in the back of the gown. Her makeup was more dramatic than she usually wore to the office and her legs were bare, and on glorious show, the dress barely skimming her knees. And they were amazing legs.

Gage's libido kicked into gear, a reminder that he hadn't had sex in a very long time. But business had been intense and when he hadn't been focused on his various building projects he'd been handling Madeline's big move into her new, off-campus apartment. An apartment she hadn't wanted, because she couldn't afford it herself. But there was no way he was letting his little sister live in a dangerous part of town, not when he could afford to buy her any home she might want. But she was stubborn, and while he appreciated that aspect of her personality, it could also be a major pain. It was also time-consuming and detrimental to his sex life.

But that was why he was now standing in the foyer of the San Diego Aquarium eyeing his PR specialist's legs.

He put his hand on the curve of her bare back and he felt her jump beneath his touch. A slow smile curved his lips. He leaned in and her sweet feminine scent teased his sense. "You wore navy blue because I told you not to wear black, didn't you?"

She pursed her lips and looked to the side, her expression defiant and sexy at the same time. "Maybe."

"Because you like to challenge me without defying me outright," he said, his lips brushing her ear. He felt the small tremor that shook her body. Interesting. She wasn't as icy as she wanted him, and people in general, to believe.

"I don't want to get fired," she whispered, her dark eyes warning him to back up or lose a limb.

He frowned. He liked the feisty edge that Lily had, but she was his employee and he had no right to touch her simply because he felt an attraction. She was a good employee, and everything that made her so great to work with, made her the kind of woman he never wanted to get involved with.

He dropped his hand and studied her flawless face. She looked different out of her work suits, with her brown curls shimmering over her shoulder. Softer. Touchable.

His hands itched to do just that. To touch her petal-soft skin, to run his fingers through her hair. His body tightened in response to the thought, even as his mind rejected it.

"As if I would fire you," he said, putting distance between them. "You know too much."

"I think I might get that matted and framed. High praise indeed."

They walked into the main section of the art exhibit, which was being held in the kelp forest. The entire room was cast in a bluish glow, compliments of the massive, three-story cylindrical aquarium that made up the structure of the space. Water plants grew to impossible heights and fish wove through them. Art was placed on easels around the room, with a place to write down and submit bids next to each one of them.

Gage walked over to one of the displays and, without even glancing at the artwork, took a form and wrote an astronomical sum on it before dropping it in the box.

"You really should be less discreet when you do things like that, and when you do things like create wildlife preserves near your resort sites," she said.

"Why is that?"

"It would help your image. And you need it. 'Property developer' is kind of a tough profession to sell to the public. You could make my job easier by trumpeting charitable contributions."

He frowned. "You were a witness. Trumpet it."

"You don't want me to, though."

His jaw tensed. "Giving for the sake of your reputation is just paying for good publicity."

"Most people don't have a problem with that."

"And what's your opinion on it, Lily? And don't give me your 'my opinion doesn't matter as long as the public likes you' speech."

She bit her lip. This side of Gage always confused Lily. In some ways he seemed more uncomfortable having people know anything good about him. He didn't seem to mind the negative press that came when he dated one supermodel, then switched to an actress the next night. But he didn't seem to want to let anyone know about his good behavior. And there was something about that that made her almost like him sometimes, and that made all the other physical things he made her feel intensify.

"It's…okay, events like this are definitely a little bit fake. It's see and be seen. Most people are flashing their bids all over the place." She jerked her head toward the glittering celebrities and debutantes gathered around different pieces of art, waving their bids around while they talked.

"I don't play the game," he said. "It doesn't appeal."

"You have to play the game a little bit, Gage. It's good for business."

"What's it like for you, doing a job that's so at odds with who you are?"

The question was so strange and unexpected, she turned sharply, her mouth dropping open. "I…how is it at odds with who I am?" She knew better than most how important image was.

The Lily Ford from a Kansas trailer park, who had pulled her way from poverty and put her past far, far behind her, was not going to get anywhere in the field of public relations. She knew, she'd tried that. But the Lily Ford who knew how to present herself with icy cool dignity, the Lily who wore tailored, designer clothing and always had her hair done perfectly, *that* Lily was a success. And it had all been a matter of image.

Who she was underneath didn't matter to clients or to the public when she was making a statement. All that mattered was what they saw. That philosophy was how she made her living, and she believed it, lived it, more than anyone she'd ever come into contact with.

"You seem to value some sort of integrity. And you believe that these sorts of shows of wealth and generosity are false. But you wish I would engage in them."

She shrugged. "If the world were different, maybe these things wouldn't matter. But we're in a media-obsessed culture. That means making a good face to present to the media, and through that, the public."

"I don't like to pander to the public."

"I know you don't, but you do like to make money. And that means keeping your image favorable. Again, easier said than done for a capitalist pig like yourself."

He shot her a deadly look that she ignored.

They continued to walk through the room. She noticed how, though Gage greeted people casually, he seemed separate from them, too. He didn't really engage with people. She made her money partly by reading people, she had to have a good idea of who her clients were and what made them tick. But after four months, in a lot of ways, Gage remained a question mark. She spent nearly every day with him, but even with that, she knew very little about him personally.

The conversation they'd just had was probably the most revealing one she'd ever had with him. Otherwise it was confined to business.

Gage knew how to play the game. He said the right things to the right people, but there was nothing personal in the way he spoke to anyone. It was the first time she'd realized that even she had never seen past Gage's public persona.

A thin blonde socialite with cleavage spilling over the top of her dress grabbed Gage by the arm and beamed up at him, seemingly oblivious to the fact that Lily was standing on the other side of him.

"Gage," the blonde said breathlessly. "I'm so glad I saw you here. There's dancing out in the courtyard," she added.

She noticed that Gage didn't bother with his signature smile. "Thank you. I'll be sure to dance with my date." He hooked his arm around her waist and slid his fingers over her hip, the light touch sending heat ripping through her body. When he brought her close to his side her legs felt as if they might buckle.

She'd never in her life been affected by a man's touch like that. Of course, that could be because she rarely let men touch her. She'd watched her mother go through an endless succession of men. Men who had asked her mother to uproot them and move from one town to another, men who had berated and belittled both of them, men who had always held the control over both of their lives. Lily had never wanted that. By the time she was thirteen she'd decided that from what she'd seen of relationships she wanted nothing to do with them.

She'd finally left home at seventeen and moved to California. Ten years later she had her own business, a beautiful apartment, complete control over her own life, and still no man. She had never regretted it. Some of her friends thought she was crazy, and insisted she was missing out on one of life's fundamental experiences. But every time she agreed to go on a date with some guy her friends promised would be perfect for her, she found herself dissecting his behavior, imagined how the possessive hand on the curve of her back would change to a fist intent on controlling her once the newness of the relationship wore off. She didn't have second dates.

It was fine for her friends. Fine for other women who

hadn't seen the steady digression of a relationship over and over again.

But Gage's touch didn't make her think of being controlled. She couldn't think of anything. All she could feel was the gentle sweep of his fingers over the curve of her hip.

"Care to dance?" he asked, his lips close to her ear, her body responding so eagerly she felt certain he would be able to see just how much he was affecting her. Her breasts felt heavy and she was thankful for her moment of near-defiance in purchasing the navy blue. Hopefully it would help conceal her tightened nipples.

The blonde was giving her a glare that had the potential to turn a lesser woman to stone, and her pride only left her with one answer to give Gage. "Of course," she said.

In a moment of total madness, she reached up and touched his face, the dark stubble there scraping her palm. Her heart hammered hard, her throat suddenly dry. She dropped her hand back to her side. She'd thought about touching his face before. Fleeting moments that had invaded her thoughts while she fought for sleep at night, fantasies that had now bled over into reality. Her palm still burned.

She followed him through the hallway lined with more aquariums and out into one of the outdoor courtyards where a band was playing.

He took her hand, lacing his fingers through hers and drawing her into his body, his expression intense. Her heart was thundering in her chest now, and there was no pretending that what she felt wasn't attraction. The most acute, real, dangerous attraction she'd ever felt in her life.

"This is inappropriate," she said, horribly conscious

of the fact that her voice felt as shaky and jittery as her whole body felt.

"Would you rather I danced with Cookie?"

She snorted a laugh, then covered her mouth with the hand that had been resting on his shoulder. She lowered it when she caught her breath, not sure whether or not she should put it back on him. "That's not really her name is it?"

"It might be a nickname, I'm not sure."

"You never asked?"

"It wasn't important at the time."

That spoke volumes about the way Gage treated relationships. He avoided commitment with flings. She avoided relationships by not having romantic contact with men altogether. But they were both avoidance tactics. In that, at least, they obviously saw eye-to-eye. Relationships were overrated.

Gage put his hand on the small of her back, on her bare skin, and he felt a small shiver go through her whole body. She was feeling every bit of the attraction he was. Strange, because he had only ever seen her in her buttoned-up professional mode, now suddenly she was unbuttoned and very, very hot. Although, she'd always been hot. He'd thought more than once about uncoiling her tightly wound hair and watching the dark curls tumble down.

She shifted against him, her hip brushing his body intimately. His muscles tensed and desire roared through him, his body hardening at the accidental contact.

He drew her closer, letting her feel. Letting her know exactly what she was doing to him. He didn't hit on employees as a rule, ever. But she tempted him. And that was a new experience. Women appealed to him, and he desired them. But he'd never considered them a serious temptation. If it wasn't the right time, it was easy for him to leave his date standing on the doorstep and go home without taking her to bed. There had been a lot of times in his life when pleasure had had to be deferred due to responsibility, either because of his family or because of business. He was an expert at deferring pleasure if necessary. But this feeling, this hot surge of lust coursing through him, didn't feel like something that could be deferred or denied.

Her head jerked up, her dark eyes wide, her breath coming in short bursts. "That's definitely not appropriate," she whispered.

"Maybe not, but I'm enjoying it."

She licked her lips, the slow, sensual movement hitting him like a punch to the gut. She looked down again, not saying anything, but leaning in a little bit closer, her breasts brushing his chest.

Her eyes fluttered closed, her lips parted slightly and she swayed a bit in his arms. Then she went stiff, pulled back quickly, her brown eyes huge with shock.

"Did you make all the bids you were planning on making?" she asked, her breasts rising and falling with her labored breathing.

"Yes," he said, trying to ignore the ache of unsatisfied desire that was gnawing at him.

"Then we should go. We'll probably have another early morning."

She turned and walked back into the building. He shook his head. She was right to have stopped things, as much as his body rebelled against the admission. He valued her too much as an employee to sacrifice it for sex. Even if it would be incredibly hot sex.

He liked to keep his life compartmentalized. There

was work, there was his family life, and then there was his sex life, and he didn't combine them. Ever.

Though with the memory of her in his arms, how soft and sweet she'd felt there, how close he had come to tasting her lips, it was hard to remember why that was.

Lily couldn't sleep, and it was all Gage's fault. And hers. He'd nearly kissed her. *She'd* nearly kissed him. Curiosity. That was all it had been. The need to know what it would be like. She'd wondered about it. She wouldn't be human if she hadn't.

Gage was so much more than any other man she'd ever met. More successful, more driven. And those were things that appealed to her. But she had never felt so compelled to abandon all of her tightly held business principles for a few moments of…of…lust.

She hadn't wanted to pull away, hadn't felt like he was trying to manipulate her in any way. She'd felt… passion. For the first time in her life she'd experienced real, physical passion. She'd always felt passion for her work, a drive and a need to succeed, but that was where it had been contained.

Her body still felt hot and restless, unfulfilled.

"I don't want Gage," she told her empty bedroom. "I don't."

He was her boss. If she wanted a relationship, which she definitely didn't, it wouldn't be with him. Her job was too important to risk it by blurring personal and professional lines. It had never been an issue for her before.

Her clients had been almost exclusively men, and even when they'd shown interest, like Jeff Campbell, she hadn't been remotely tempted to accept. There was a clear line drawn in her mind. Work was work.

She clenched and unclenched her fists, trying to make the shaky feeling go away. The worst thing wasn't that Gage was her boss, it was how out of control he'd made her feel. She'd kissed men before—several of them—and the experience had ranged from completely undesirable to okay. None had lit her on fire from the inside out. But the near kiss with Gage made her feel like she was burning.

The worst thing was that she knew that if his lips had touched hers, that last shred of sanity would have turned to a vapor and any inclination she had to resist him would be gone with it. And when had she ever struggled with her willpower? She created her own destiny. She was in charge of her own life.

She let out a low growl of frustration and tossed off her covers before stalking over to her computer. If she wasn't going to get sleep, she would get work done.

She opened up her email account and clicked open the message that she knew contained her search engine alerts on Forrestation Inc. and Gage Forrester. It was important for her to keep tabs on what was being said about him so she could release a statement if necessary.

She scanned the message and her stomach dropped. She bit out a curse and picked up her phone, speed dialing Gage's number, not caring that it was three in the morning.

"Gage, we have a very serious problem."

CHAPTER FOUR

"THIS is garbage." Gage threw the printed papers back down on his desk, his muscles tense, his entire body wound up and ready to attack at any moment.

Hearing Maddy's voice, thick with tears on the other end of the phone a few moments before, had made him feel capable of very serious violence against the person responsible for spreading such venomous rumors.

It made him feel physically ill, seeing the article written with such foul accusations. Accusations directed at Madeline. She was doing well now, had graduated from college, was finally coming out of her shell and putting their neglectful childhood being her. She'd been such a quiet little girl, as if she was afraid to step out of line. Afraid he might abandon her, too. But she'd grown so much in the past few years, and now this threatened to destroy everything Maddy had battled so hard for.

"I agree," Lily said. "It's not news, and it's a shame we live in a culture that thinks it is. But the simple fact is that we do, and this story is going to be in every print and digital publication this morning, from respected newspaper to scandal rag."

"She doesn't need this. She's been through enough. She just graduated. It's hard enough finding a job, and she won't let me help her. Add this, and no one will hire her."

Lily sucked in a sharp breath and tugged on her suit jacket. "I know, Gage. Trust me. I'm fully aware of how hard it is to be a woman in the corporate world, and a…" She looked at him, her expression filled with distaste. "Sorry, but a sex scandal is hard to move past. For the woman, at least."

"She wasn't involved with him," Gage growled, skimming the article on the top of the stack again. "She swears she wasn't. She says he was her boss, she was doing an unpaid internship, and he came on to her. She refused to sleep with him, and now, now that his wife is leaving him because he's a lecherous old jackass, he's blaming Maddy to try and make her look like she was some kind of predatory female out to destroy their marriage, out to take him down and ruin his life."

"Regardless of whether she had a relationship with him or not…"

Gage's heart thundered harder, rage pounding through him. "She didn't."

Lily put her hands up in a gesture of surrender. "Okay, you know your sister better than I do, if you say she didn't, she didn't. But now that it's out like this…there's very little we can do to fight it. It's going to be everywhere. Even if she were to come back with her own version of the story, which I think she should do in the future no matter what, this is going to hit like an explosion. William Callahan is so high-profile…and his wife—soon to be ex-wife—is more famous than he is."

Gage was familiar with the man's trophy wife. She'd come on to him at several industry parties, and, despite the fact that she was a world-famous model whose looks had, literally, been memorialized in song, he'd never even been tempted. He didn't poach other men's wives. He didn't need to. But she was definitely open to playing around behind her husband's back, and clearly Mr. Callahan was no better. And they were trying to drag his sister into their sordid lives.

"Infamous is more like it," he bit out. "I'll ruin him for this."

"I don't blame you, Gage, I don't, but before you engage in serious ruination, we need to figure out how we're going to handle the media firestorm Madeline is about to get hit by."

Lily had met Maddy on a few occasions. She was a pretty brunette, petite and fine-boned, delicate and small, none of the height Gage had inherited passed down to her. She looked young, and in some ways seemed younger. It was obvious that Gage doted on her, and that, despite that, Madeline made an effort to be independent, which Lily completely respected.

She also understood the kind of dilemma she found herself in. It was hard for a woman to be taken seriously in business. It was hard to find the right balance. Dress up too much, men make assumptions about what you're there for…not enough and you would get torn apart by the other women.

"We can create our own distraction."

Lily narrowed her eyes. "No. I don't know what you're thinking, I just know it's probably going to create a big cleanup for me."

He shook his head. "It won't. But it will take the focus off of Maddy. If we can bury this story with one of our own, it will at least soften the blow."

"You have a valid point, but I seriously doubt you're

going to magically stumble upon something that over-shadows a scandal of this magnitude."

"I thought I might announce my impending marriage."

Her eyebrows shot up. "Marriage? You aren't getting married."

"No. But don't you think it would make a nice headline?"

She let out a completely undignified, involuntary snort. "No one would believe it."

"You don't think so?"

"No. You're not exactly the marrying kind."

"And why is that?"

"Marriage requires monogamy," she said. At least it was supposed to require monogamy. She'd witnessed all the drama that came when people strayed. Her mother had thrived on the drama, the jealousy...

"I don't cheat on women. If I'm attracted to someone else, I end the relationship I'm in. I see no point in pretending to want one woman if I want another."

"You seem to change the woman you want with alarming frequency."

"And that's why it would be such a big story if I were preparing to get married. I've dated enough actresses and models to have serious headline appeal with the tabloids."

"Okay, yeah, I'll give you that. But where are you going to find a woman who won't want to marry you for real? One who will keep her mouth shut about the arrangement."

She looked back at Gage—his blue eyes were trained on her and a slow smile spread over his handsome face.

"Lily."

She didn't like the way he said her name, with intent, his low voice rolling over it, making it sound like a verbal caress. And it made her stomach tighten and her breasts feel heavy. Like last night. Like when he'd held her in his arms.

"I want you to marry me."

She could only stare at him. Words were failing her, which was virtually unheard-of. She always knew what to say. She always knew how to respond in every situation, quickly and efficiently, cutting if necessary. She was never speechless. Except she was now.

She opened her mouth, then shut it again, trying desperately to think of some kind of sharp, witty response. Instead she settled for simple. "Not really, though."

A short chuckle escaped his lips. "No. Not really. I just want you to be my fiancée."

"No." She shook her head. "No! Absolutely not."

"How much do you value your job, Lily?"

She locked her teeth together. "It's everything to me. I've worked very hard to get where I am."

"It would be a shame to have any of your hard work compromised, wouldn't it?"

"Yes," she bit out.

"I don't want Madeline's hard work compromised because she got tossed to the wolves. I don't want her to lose all of the progress she's made, all of the confidence she's managed to gain."

The threat, though he didn't state it explicitly, was certainly implied. If she wanted to keep her job, she had to play by his rules.

"And it has to be you," he continued. "You and I were seen together at the gala last night, and we were definitely breaching the boundaries of professionalism."

"We were well within normal boundaries of a boss

and employee attending an event together," she said, even as images of him holding her close flashed through her mind.

He raised his eyebrows. "Really? What else do you consider within normal employer-employee boundaries? Gotten engaged to any of your other bosses?"

"I haven't even agreed to get engaged to this one," she said through clenched teeth.

On a personal level, she was horrified by the idea. She didn't want to spend more time with Gage. She didn't want to pretend to be his adoring fiancée. But if she pushed that aside and looked at it objectively, she knew that this was the best way to throw the spotlight off of Madeline without completely compromising Gage's public image.

"You're right," she said finally. "I hate it when you're right."

"This will be simple for you, Lily. You're the consummate professional."

"If you think I'm going to fall for that, you're sadly delusional."

"What is that?" he asked, leaning back in his chair, hands behind his head, showing off his wonderful arm muscles. He knew.

"You're turning on the Forrester charm. It doesn't work on me," she said, even as her stomach tightened a little bit.

"All right, then forget the charm. We don't have another choice. If I go down, you go down with me. We have to fix this. If you walk away, it only gets worse for you. No one will hire you if they find out you left a client in the lurch when a massive scandal was breaking that related to his family. If you help successfully diffuse this, though…"

"I know." She would most likely be sworn to se-
crecy about the fine details, but she imagined she would
earn herself an extremely glowing reference. And the
best record for a PR specialist was, without a doubt,
a smooth history with the press. More than a hint of
scandal and her career was in serious danger. "Fine.
Yes."

"Excellent." Gage picked up his mobile phone and
punched in a number. "Dave? I need an engagement
ring. I don't know." He looked at her. "What size ring
do you wear?"

"A six."

"Six." He paused. "It doesn't matter. Make sure it's
noticeable." He snapped the phone shut.

"Did you just call poor David at five in the morning
to have him buy me a ring?"

"You already know the answer, why did you even
ask?"

Annoyance rolled in her stomach, along with nerves
that refused to be calmed. She flexed her fingers, imagining the weight of a ring there. His ring. It made everything in her feel jittery. It was such a symbol of
ownership. Like he was marking her as his. Which was
silly because they weren't in a real relationship and they
were never going to be. But everything about marriage
and relationships severely unnerved her, and it was hard
to shake the anxiety that was coursing through her.

"I was just incredulous," she snapped.

"So, what's the story?"

Right. Work. This she could do. Create a press
release, get the right spin. She was good at this. She
grabbed her notebook of the desk. "We've been working
together for a while. We've grown closer, friendship,
then, well…more. And then you proposed last night

after the gala, which is why I didn't have a ring yet. Because that detail would have been noticed."

"Good. Take care of it. The ring will be in your office in less than an hour then you can make the announcement."

She could tell by the way he was sitting, looking at her, that she was dismissed. "As proposals go," she said, unable to resist, "that one ranks right up there with a ring in the food."

"I thought women liked that," he said, his slightly amused.

"No. It gets the ring messy and if you don't find it you might break a tooth."

"I'll keep that in mind should I ever stage a real proposal."

"Do you actually plan on doing that?" she asked, not able to picture it.

"I don't plan to, no."

"I didn't think so."

"What about you? You're impervious to wedding bells, so you say, but do you have a boyfriend you're going to have to explain this to?"

"No. And even if I did, I told you when you hired me, work comes first. I was serious."

"You would ditch your boyfriend to further your career?"

"Yes," she said, without hesitation. "Don't tell me you wouldn't do the same to any of your past lovers."

"Of course I would. But most women don't see things that way."

"I'll ignore the most comment for now and just say, then maybe some women don't have a problem with someone else having so much control over their life, but I do. My career is important to me. It comes first.

If I was with someone, he would have to understand that."

"No man is going to understand you playing fiancée to someone else."

"Then I guess there isn't a right man for me," she said, smiling tightly. "Not in a permanent sense anyway." She couldn't resist adding it, because the last thing she wanted was to betray the fact that she didn't do relationships of any sort, at all, full stop, ever. And why should it matter if Gage knew? She didn't usually worry about it at all. In fact, she was extremely secure in her antirelationship status.

"I don't see there being a right woman for me in that way, either. Which, ironically, makes us perfectly compatible."

A reluctant smile tugged at her lips. "I suppose, ironically, that's very true."

"Now go, prepare a statement. We'll make a formal announcement this morning. Start calling media outlets and let them know we have a story. The more of them we can distract the better."

She nodded once. She could do this. It was her job. That was all. It was only business, nothing more, there was no reason why it would feel like anything else.

She clenched her hands into fists, trying not to imagine what the weight of the ring would feel like, then turned and went back to her office.

The frenetic energy of a press conference was usually something Lily thrived on. She loved everything about them. The noise, the chaos, the low hum of excitement that pulsed through the crowd. She was never nervous. She always knew just what she was going to say, or what her client was going to say.

But this morning, she felt as if she was going to throw up.

Gage took her hand and a flash of heat raced up through her fingers and into her whole body, warming her core, making her heart beat faster. She wished she could blame that on the press conference, but she couldn't. Gage had an unexpected, unaccountable effect on her body. One that made her feel like she was out of control, which she hated more than anything.

He tugged on her lightly and led her up the stairs and to the podium. Gage held her hand up and moved it out toward the light so that the massive ring, which she had placed on her own finger only a few minutes earlier, caught the light. The noise in the crowd quieted, everyone staring at them, their eyes expectant, hungry for a story.

"Thank you all for coming this morning," Gage said, lowering their hands. "Before any rumors started flying, we wanted to make a formal announcement. I've asked my public relations specialist, Lily Ford, to marry me and she's accepted."

Then, like an invisible barrier was broken, flashes from cameras went off and questions started flying at them from all directions.

"Mr. Forrester, is this in any way related to the news story about your sister this morning?"

She could feel Gage tense, his hand squeezing hers tightly. Reflexively, she reached over with her other hand and traced her fingers lightly over his knuckles.

"We are not discussing my sister or the blatant untruths that were printed about her, any more questions along that line and we're finished here."

The sound of his voice acted like a high beam in the fog of her brain. She jerked her hand away from his, horrified that she'd touched him like that. Like she had permission to do it, like it was natural.

"Do you have a date set?" This came from a woman in the crowd.

"We're still looking at venues," Lily responded.

"And what does this mean for your dating life?" one of the men asked.

"This means he's through with dating," Lily said sharply. Usually she was very cool in these situations, but she greatly resented the excessive interest in the lives of public figures anyway, and being at the center of it only added to the resentment.

"She's right about that," Gage said, drawing his thumb over the back of her hand, sending little ripples of sensation through her. "I never thought I would get married. But when I met Lily... Well, she's all that I want." He looked up, his blue eyes intent on hers. Her breath caught. He looked like he meant every word he'd just spoken, his expression sincere, his eyes trained only on her. No mystery why he scored so many beautiful women with such ease. He could do romance without breaking a sweat, and he could sound completely honest while speaking words that were nothing more than beautiful lies.

And the worst thing was that, even knowing that, even having a complete and total man embargo, it affected her. Her heart was thundering, her stomach tight, her breasts heavy.

And when his eyes dropped and his focus moved to her lips, she was silently hoping he would lean in and close the distance between them.

She shook her head sharply and tried to force the image out of her mind. She didn't want to kiss him. He was charming her. Like he'd done to thousands of other women multiple thousands of times. But she wasn't like those other women. She had standards. She knew what happened when you let a man in like that, when you gave someone else so much power in your life. She would never make that mistake. Her life was just as she liked it. Well-ordered and entirely in her control.

The rest of the questions went by in a blur and she stood there, smiling, her face placid, her manner serene. She was a professional at projecting calm when her thoughts were churning beneath the surface.

Everything in her was concentrating on ignoring the place where Gage was touching her, on where he was moving his thumb over the sensitive skin on her hand. On the heat that coursed through her from such a simple, nonsexual touch.

"Thank you, we won't be taking any more questions. We both have some work to get back to, and I'd hate to have to fire my fiancée." The crowd laughed softly at his joke. Lily tightened her lips to try and avoid grimacing.

He led her off of the stage and the minute they were safely ensconced in his limousine she jerked her hand away from him, rubbing at the spot he'd been brushing with his thumb.

"Try not to act like my touch offends you next time," he said.

She tilted her head up to face him and immediately wished she hadn't. The impact of him, his blue eyes narrowed, his expression hard, was more than she'd anticipated. After working with Gage for four months she should be used to him by now, but, while he was always in charge, no doubt about it, he didn't usually give off that level of intensity. He was completely serious about his work, but beneath it all was a definite security. He wasn't the kind of man who had to posture and get worked up over every minor detail in order to project his power. Never had she felt a hint of the intensity that she knew was just beneath the surface right now.

She knew he loved his sister, knew he was protective of her, but she hadn't realized just how much.

"I didn't act like your touch offended me," she said, looking out the window at the harbor, watching the white boats blur together. "I was perfectly composed."

"And stiff."

This was not a new refrain. She couldn't even recall the number of times she'd been called frigid, on those ill-fated, unwanted dates that had been concocted by her well-meaning friends.

Stiff was actually a little bit nicer, but she imagined the sentiment was much the same.

"Sorry, I'll work on my fawning."

"Do that," he said, his voice icy.

"No one else could tell. And if they could they would attribute it to nerves from being in front of a crowd."

"You make statements to the press on an almost daily basis."

"True," she admitted, "but not personal statements. Maybe I'm private."

"You are very tight-lipped about your personal life."

Personal life? That would be a fun conversation. The gym four nights a week. A health-conscious meal for one, and then whatever show she felt like watching on TV since there was never anyone there to complain. If she didn't have issues with pet hair she would probably have a cat, which would at least give her companion-ship, but would give him unfair ammo against her.

"That's why they call it a personal life, Gage, although clearly you didn't get the memo."

"Tell me this, Lily, is there any point for me to try and hide my personal life? You know how the media is, and if you aren't up front about what goes on behind closed doors they make it up, or someone makes it up for them."

"Okay, I see your point. But you tend to…flaunt."

"No, I happen to date women who are as high profile as I am, and that makes us targets. We go out, and that seems to constitute as news. We can't stay in my bedroom all the time."

The way he said that, his husky voice low and intimate in the confines of the limo, made her heart rate skyrocket. Why, *why* was he able to this to her? Why did he have the power to fill her head with images of tangled limbs and the sounds of heavy breathing, the scent of sweat-slicked bodies? Men, in a real life, personal sense, never did that to her.

She liked men, she just liked them from a distance. Like in the pages of a glossy magazine or on a movie screen. She had a sex drive, just like most everyone else, but in actual, personal application…that was what made her feel anxious. Which wasn't conducive to arousal. Orgasm required a loss of control she couldn't fathom being able to achieve, or even wanting to achieve, with another person.

But it was as if Gage was able to bypass all of her natural issues, all of her closely guarded reserve, and make her want things she'd never anticipated having a desire for. It wasn't a matter of wanting to abolish her personal barriers so that she could experience real desire and satisfaction with Gage, it was a matter of them seeming to dissolve and her desperately wishing they would return. He was her boss, and work was too important to even consider engaging in an affair that would damage that.

Fine for some women to have flings and keep themselves emotionally separate, but she was afraid she wasn't one of those women. Her mother certainly wasn't. Every man she ever slept with consumed everything she had. All her emotion, all her time, her self-respect. It had made growing up a living hell for Lily. There had been nothing she could do at the time, but now, it was up to her how she ran her life, and she chose to maintain total control.

End of story. So her hormones could just deal with it.

"I don't suppose you can," she said, teeth clenched.

"Check your alerts," he said, back to his high-handed self.

She took her phone out of her pocket and pulled up her email. She'd received a few email alerts, letting her know Gage's name had popped up in search engines. She opened the first one. "It looks like our engagement is big news. Huge news, in fact."

"How about Maddy?"

"The story's still there, and I wouldn't call it buried," she said, looking through the pages of search results. "But it's quieted."

"Good," he said.

Gage took his phone from his jacket pocket and dialed Maddy, setting the mobile to speakerphone. "Are you all right?" he asked.

"Yes, Gage. I'm fine."

She didn't sound distraught, but he could tell she'd been crying, which made his stomach tighten. "It's handled."

"I saw that," she said. "I don't want you doing this for me. I'm an adult, Gage. I have to clean up my own messes."

"Not this one, Maddy. Callahan is a bastard to drag you into this, and it's way out of your league. Let me handle it."

"Gage, you have to let me stand on my own some-time."

"I know," he said, his chest tightening. "After this."

He knew Maddy was an adult, and he understood her feeling like she needed to fight her own battles, and, if he was honest, he was more than ready to have a little less involvement with her life. But he wasn't letting her deal with this on her own.

"I'm sending you over to the Swiss resort for a couple of weeks. Just until all of this dies down."

"Gage…"

"Maddy, let me fix it."

He heard her heavy sigh on the other end of the phone. "Okay, Gage, I'll go to Switzerland. Are you still going through with your fake engagement?"

"How do you know it's fake?" he asked, looking over at Lily, who was still staring out the window, trying to ignore him. Her slight shoulders were set rigidly, her long, stocking-clad legs crossed. And they were extremely fine legs. Lily wasn't very tall, she barely skimmed his shoulder, even in her man-slaying stilettos, but those legs were long and shapely, just begging for him to run his hands over them, to draw one up so that she had it wrapped around him, bringing her closer so that he could…

He slammed a mental door on his errant fantasy.

"Because she isn't your type at all. She's too…stuffy," Maddy said.

Lily's head whipped around, brown eyes wide, full lips pinched. He swore and punched the speaker button off. "Enjoy Switzerland, Maddy. Let me handle the rest."

He snapped the phone shut. Lily was looking away again, her focus very firmly on the scenery out the window.

He wanted to touch her. To see if he could make her melt. To see what it would take to get her to loosen her hair, to get her to unbutton a little bit. Or all the way. It was easy for him to picture her naked, her perfect, petite body on display for him. She was so pale…the thought of all that milky white skin contrasting against his black sheets was the most erotic fantasy his subconscious had ever created for him.

Two things kept him from exploring the fantasy. First, she was an employee, and that was a no-go as far as he was concerned. Second, she had *serious* written all over her. He didn't do serious. Not in his sexual relationships. He'd done serious. Not in romantic relationships, but his entire childhood and young adult years had been nothing but responsibility.

His mother had done okay raising him to a point, but Maddy had been a late-in-life surprise, and his mother hadn't been willing to miss more years on the job to raise a child she hadn't wanted. His father had always put his career first and had even less time for Maddy. And that left him. He was fifteen years older and more than capable of caring for her.

When he was twenty-five, just out of college and making his first million in property development, Maddy had called and told him it had been three days since anyone had been home, and she hadn't had anything to eat. He'd gone to get her and she'd lived with him from the age of ten until she'd gone to college. That was a lot of serious for a confirmed bachelor who had his own career to try and build. Fortunately, he'd had a network of good friends that had helped him try to balance work and what basically amounted to sudden parenthood.

He didn't resent it and he would never have given it up for anything, but he was done with that. In his estimation, he'd raised a child, when he'd been much too young to do it, and he had no intention of going there again. He'd already dealt with the angst of a teenage girl's first crush, threatened her dates with bodily harm if they laid a hand on her, helped her find a dress for prom, then seen her off to college.

And despite the fact that Lily certainly didn't seem like the kind of woman who had a biological clock ticking, she still read serious. She didn't date very often and she was probably the kind of woman that took a certain amount of seduction before she engaged in a physical relationship.

He preferred women who were fun and uncomplicated, and if that made him shallow in the eyes of the press, that was fine with him. He was the one who had to live his life, and as long as he was happy with it, he didn't concern himself with the opinions of others.

Except when it came to Maddy.

"So, now what? We have to go to galas together?" Lily asked, her voice dry. What Maddy had said bothered her that was obvious. And if she hadn't been so very off-limits he would have offered comfort. But he only knew two ways to do that. One was parental, and one was decidedly not. He imagined neither would be welcome.

"I was thinking a romantic getaway," he said, enjoying the way her lips tightened further. He wasn't used to seeing Lily flustered, but she was exactly that about the whole situation.

"And what about our jobs?"

"It will be a working getaway of course. I was planning on going to Thailand to check on the resort progress sometime in the next week. And now seems like a perfect time. Maddy's in Switzerland until the story blows over, and she'll be at one of my resorts, so the security will be tight, and with that taken care of, we can get publicity for the resort."

"And for us," Lily returned dryly.

"Doesn't hurt."

Lily's heart beat faster. Curse the man. "If Maddy is taken care of…"

"We still have to see this through. If you're caught lying so blatantly, your credibility will be destroyed. Along with the rest of your career."

And curse him again, he was right. That was always the risk with this job. There was a fine line between bending the truth and outright lies. She avoided lies whenever she could, but ultimately, her client's image— or in this case, his sister's— was her concern. But if she was caught being…economical…with the truth, the media would never take her seriously again. Credibility, once it was damaged like that, was not an easy thing to repair.

"Point taken." She put her smile on, the one she reserved for press conferences. "I guess we're going to Thailand."

CHAPTER FIVE

It was late when Gage's private plane landed on the island of Koh Samui. A car was waiting for them when they got off of the plane. Lily expected nothing less. Gage was always efficient. Or at least, the people he hired were always completely efficient. Which, she imagined, brought it back around to Gage being efficient.

She took a deep breath of the humid, salty air before getting into the limo.

Gage settled in beside her. His top button was undone, his tie long discarded, his sleeves pushed up over his elbows, revealing tanned, muscular forearms that demanded an in-depth study from female admirers. He still smelled good, too, even after long hours of travel.

"Don't you find the limo a bit cliché?" she asked, running her hands unconsciously over the cool leather.

"I find it practical. I have a driver, I have privacy. I have enough room to work—" he looked at her, his blue eyes hot "—or play."

She held up a hand and tried to ignore the chip in her manicure. "I don't need to hear about your backseat exploits."

He reached across the seats and gripped the clip that

was holding her bun in place, letting her brown hair fall around her in a heavy curtain. He slid his fingers through it, rubbing the tender places that were sore from so many hours pinned back. The gentle pressure of his fingers felt so good. It was part massage, part sexual tease. She wanted to tilt her head and lean into his touch. To moan in ecstasy over what he was making her feel.

Instead she jerked her head away from his touch. "Why did you do that?"

"You may not want to discuss any of my backseat exploits, but if there are reporters waiting at the resort it wouldn't hurt you to look as though you'd been engaging in some of your own." He drew his thumb lightly over her cheek. "You're already flushed."

She let her breath out slowly. "It's hot."

His blue eyes were serious, studying, and she felt her face get even hotter. "Yes. It is." He moved away from her, leaning back against the seat.

"How is the building project going?" she asked. Anything to break the tension that had just stretched between them, so real and tight that it had seemed like a physical force. It was worse that she was sure he felt it.

But then he was a man, and she was a woman, so, naturally, if she was giving off any attraction vibes he was going to pick up on them and reciprocate. It was the way it worked. A woman didn't need to be especially desirable, only available.

"It's going well. Most of the individual villas are up and ready for use. The main portion of the resort is still under construction, but I've made sure that the villa we're staying in is totally stocked, and some of the housekeeping staff I've already hired are staying on site, so they'll be around to take care of our needs."

"I don't need housekeeping," she said dryly. "How do you think I manage in my daily life?"

"I assumed you were busy and you would have some domestic help."

Which would require her to allow a stranger in her house. Which might seem fanatical to some, but she'd done cramped, shared communal living with her mother and whatever man of the month her mother was currently attached to. No privacy. And some of the men had attempted to take advantage…it was no wonder she'd never been the kind of woman to experiment with flings. She'd had to work too hard to maintain any sort of innocence in that environment.

"We're not all billionaires, Gage."

"But I know what I pay you," he said dryly.

"But you don't know my expenses. Maybe I own beachfront property."

"You don't."

She turned to him, eyebrows raised. "You don't think I do?"

"You're too sensible."

She smirked. "As it happens I own a beachfront condo."

The West Coast, the ocean, had been her dream growing up. She'd seen the ocean for the first time at seventeen, when she moved to California, and it had been her goal to be able to see it from her bedroom window. It had taken quite a few years, but eighteen months ago she'd finally gotten the keys to her new beachfront home. A home she'd worked for. The home she'd earned. It had been the best feeling in the world.

The ultimate reward for her years of hard work, focus and independence.

"You don't seem the type."

"I don't?"

"Do you surf? Swim?"

She laughed. "No."

"That's why you don't seem the type."

"I used to dream about the ocean," she said without thinking. "In Kansas we have seas of cornfields. No ocean. I thought if I could see the ocean…it was like the world would be open to me. Endless possibilities on the horizons."

As soon as she finished she wished she hadn't said anything. She'd never told anyone that before, not even any of her friends. Her dreams had always been her own. She had a really nice group of friends, but they kept things casual, not really in depth. And that was how she liked things in general with people. Now she felt horribly exposed, and to Gage of all people, who always seemed like he could see into her, like he knew things about her even she didn't know.

"It's a good dream," he said. "And now you have it."

She nodded once. "Part of it."

"You want success."

"I want unsurpassed success in my field," she said.

"Something I understand."

"You have that kind of success, Gage."

He offered her a partial smile. "Yet, I still want more. It's never quite enough, that's the thing about ambition. But that's what keeps me going, and in business, you have to keep going. Money doesn't wait for you. If I wasn't building this resort, someone else would be, and it would be my missed opportunity. As it is, it's my payday and someone else's regret."

"You don't do regret, do you?" she asked.

"I make sure I never need to."

They pulled onto a road that was newer than the main highway, the pavement dark and smooth as the road curved around the base of sheer rock face covered with vines and moss. The road led up the mountain and the foliage grew thicker and greener and palm trees and other topical plants grew thick along the roadside.

It certainly hadn't been overtaken by Forrestation Inc., as some of the environmental groups had feared. With the exception of the road, Lily could barely make out any signs of civilization.

The partially built resort was at the top of the mountain, with a clear view of the crystalline ocean and the white sand beaches. Paths led from the main building and into the trees and, she assumed, to the separate teakwood villas.

The limo came to a halt and Lily got out without waiting for Gage, or the driver, to open her door for her.

"It has a view of the ocean," Gage said, coming to stand beside her.

She cleared her throat. "Yes, it does." It bothered her now, that he had that little piece of her. Now he knew what to say, and he knew why this place was so perfect to her. He would know what she was thinking.

She shrugged off the unsettling thought. "So, where am I staying?"

"We are staying in the house I had built for my own personal use."

The thought of staying with him did not settle well. "Why are we staying together?"

"The board is visiting. That means we have to look as cozy as possible."

"But it's a whole house?"

"Yes. More than three thousand square feet. You'll never have to see me. Unless you want to, of course."

The look that he gave her was so heated it made her body temperature skyrocket. His meaning wasn't implied so much as stated. Boldly, explicitly.

"I don't," she said, tight-lipped, knowing how uptight she sounded.

He lifted an eyebrow. "What if there's a business matter we need to discuss?"

"Then I'll look for you."

"What did you think I meant, Lily?"

She made a scoffing sound in the back of her throat. "You know perfectly well what…because it's what you were implying." He was flustering her. Honestly flustering her. That did not happen. Ever.

He didn't say anything. Didn't even try to break the thick silence with a clever comment. He only looked at her, his blue eyes roaming over her body, making her feel like he was undressing her. Like she was already undressed. Like he could see everything. Every flaw, every imperfection, every bit of her.

She looked away, throat dry. "Okay, so where's the house?"

"Just down the path."

He surprised her by opening the trunk of the limousine and taking their suitcases out himself before heading down the heavily wooded trail. She followed him, as best she could in her stilettos, which were not made for a natural path, however nicely constructed.

She wobbled and pitched forward, catching herself on his broad shoulders, her breasts crushed against his back. He stopped, his body stiff and strong beneath her weight. Her heart thundered heavily, both from the near fall, and from being so close to him again.

It was just like it had been when they were dancing. He was so solid, so hot and male. She wanted to melt into him. To chase after the riot of sensations that were moving through her body at lightning speed. To finally know what it meant to share sexual pleasure with someone else.

She pushed away from him, wobbling again, but she managed to get her balance on her own. She took a sharp breath. Just the small distance between them afforded her more clarity of thought. But when she touched him…she forgot everything. Everything but her steadily growing desire for him. Well, not really for him personally, but for his body. Gage was the last man on earth—okay, not really the last man but he was low on the list—with whom she would choose to have a real relationship. But something about him physically, probably his undeniable sex appeal, got to her more than any other man ever had.

It was raw and elemental, beyond common sense. And she really, really hated it.

"Sorry," she said, her voice breaking and, she knew, revealing just how much the encounter had affected her.

"Be careful," he said. His voice sounded thicker, huskier. That was when she knew. Knew that he was affected by her, too, that her touching him, pressing against him, was doing the same thing to him that it had done to her. And that did not make things better.

She twisted the engagement ring on her finger and reminded herself exactly why she didn't need a relationship, with Gage or anyone else. She didn't want anyone to *own* her. Didn't want anyone to control her and manipulate her with her own foolish emotions. She'd seen how it worked, what love did to you, what it asked of you. It wasn't anything she wanted a part of.

She followed him the rest of the way, more slowly and more carefully, until they reached the house. It was set up on stilts and made from solid dark teakwood with the traditional curves of Thai architecture, mixed with a modern sensibility. The large, covered outdoor living area that wrapped around the house made the most of the natural environment and the view. It appeared rustic in a sense, but she knew that inside it would have every modern convenience available, and even some that weren't available. Not to mere mortals anyway.

"I love it," she said, meaning it.

"I like it, too," he said. "I designed it, actually."

"You did?"

He shrugged. "That was how I got into property development. Architecture has always interested me. I like building resorts that are functional and beautiful, and blend in with the natural culture and landscape."

"You really have to start saying these things in public," she said.

Now she knew something about Gage, she realized. And he knew something about her. That caused strange tightening sensation in her chest.

"Why? Then your job would be easy."

She rolled her eyes, ignoring the persistent roll of her stomach. "Can't have that." She walked up the exterior stairs of the house without waiting for him and went inside.

It was gorgeous, the décor simple and traditional, a muted color palette that caused all attention to be drawn to the view outside, to the vivid colors of the beach that could never be rivaled by anything man-made.

She moved through the open living room and into the kitchen, which was outfitted, as she'd predicted, with top-of-the-line equipment. Stainless steel appliances and granite countertops. The kitchen flowed seamlessly into the dining room, which went back around into the living room.

"Where's my room?" she asked, starting to feel desperate for a little bit of space. He was making her whole body feel restless and jittery and she needed a break.

"Just through here," he said and gestured to another open doorway just off of the living room.

There was no door, just a cleverly angled wall that kept the bed from view. The bedroom was open to a massive bathroom that was, again, only private in part.

"Are there no interior doors in this house?" she asked, feeling panic start to pick at her calm, fraying the edges a bit.

"No. I thought it would compromise the integrity of the design."

"It compromises common decency. That's what it does. That's…that's my concern," she said, feeling her heart rate rise.

"I promise I'll keep to my quarters."

She hated that she couldn't play like she was fine with it. Another thing she was revealing about herself, which was one reason she valued her privacy so much. How many other twenty-seven-year-old women had such a hang-up about sharing space? Especially with a man. Most women her age shared space with men frequently and happily.

"I just…I live by myself for a reason."

"Really?" he asked, genuine interest in his voice.

Crap. She was sharing again. "I like privacy."

"I understand that."

Gage fully understood the need for privacy. Having a child—his sister—live with him for eight years had severely limited his privacy, dictating who he could have over and when. What sort of activities he could indulge in. Of course, now that Maddy was on her own, he could have women over if he chose to, but he'd gotten so used to going to hotels when he wanted sex that he'd never really adapted back.

And now that he had the privacy he wanted, the house felt empty sometimes. He still didn't want to share it with any of his mistresses. He didn't need women leaving toothbrushes on his sink. It was a level of commitment he had no desire to pursue. He had nothing to offer a woman beyond a little mutual fun in the bedroom, and he didn't see the point in making her believe otherwise. That was why neutral locations reigned supreme in his book.

Although, having Lily stay here with him didn't bother him at all. But then, Lily wasn't his mistress, and she also didn't seem like she knew how to cling or simper, which made her seem like a much safer houseguest.

"I live alone, too," he added.

"I like it," she said.

"So do I."

"I need a shower," she said, abruptly. Then her pale cheeks turned a delicate raspberry.

He couldn't help but picture her naked in the shower, water sluicing over all that pale skin as it grew rosy from the heat. He felt an ache start to build in his groin. Maybe she wouldn't be the most convenient houseguest.

Not if he wanted to keep things professional between them. Although he was starting to wonder why it mattered. He was trying to be decent. It seemed a little bit on the shady side to hit on a woman whose paychecks you signed. But decency was starting to seem less important.

Then she lowered her eyes, her blush intensifying, and he remembered why making a move on her was a bad idea. She wouldn't just be another good time. She was more than that. If she were the kind of woman who would have said she needed a shower and, instead of blushing, had given him a sultry look and invited him to join, then he would have been more than willing to forget professionalism then and there.

But she wasn't that woman. Despite the air of confidence she gave off most of the time, all it took was a touch, or a small moment of sexual tension, and the confidence melted away. She either stiffened and moved away or she blushed like an innocent. He didn't want to deal with any of that. He couldn't. He had plenty to offer women in the way of gifts and physical pleasure. But he didn't want marriage or love, he didn't see the point.

His career was too important, and he'd put it on the back burner for eight years. He wouldn't do it again. Not for a wife or a child. It wouldn't be fair to him, or them. A wife and child didn't deserve to be second. He and Maddy hadn't deserved to be second. But they had been. A very distant second. He refused to put a children through what his parents had subjected Maddy and him to. He wouldn't make them wonder what they could do to earn some attention, to gain a small about of their parents' interest.

That meant marriage was not an option.

"I'll meet you for dinner," he said, his voice rough with arousal.

She nodded jerkily. "Okay. See you then."

He turned to leave the room, fighting the urge to turn and take her in his arms and kiss her, to find out if she would be stiff against his lips, or if she would be soft and pliant.

He wanted her soft and pliant, more than he could remember wanting any woman in his life. It didn't matter that his head knew she was the wrong woman to get involved with. His body wanted her.

He tried to conjure up an image of Penny, his last mistress, the mistress he had parted ways with a very distant six months ago. He couldn't. The only woman his body wanted was Lily.

When Lily emerged an hour later she was back in her business attire, hair pinned back, makeup expertly applied. Her lipstick was a paler rose than her typical color, coordinating with her new manicure and her sky-high stilettos.

Her endless supply of colorful high-heeled shoes never failed to fascinate him. Her work wardrobe was neutral, black and gray, with the occasional brown. But she wore a rainbow on her feet. He'd dated women that wore shoes like that, but mixed with garish jewelry and flashy dresses. Their entire look was so obvious that nothing stood out. Lily knew how to dress for impact. And with a figure like hers, everything short of a burlap sack had pretty major impact. Although, he imagined a burlap sack might even pack a punch with Lily's curves to complement it.

"I'm ready to eat," she said.

"Dinner will be up shortly."

She narrowed her brown eyes. "I thought we were meeting with the board."

"Tomorrow. They've only just flown in and will be eating in their quarters so that they can rest."

"Considerate of you," she said, teeth gritted. "Although if I would have known we were eating in, I wouldn't have dressed for a business dinner." She was annoyed, but not necessarily about being out of the loop. Probably something to do with being alone with him.

"I think you still would have." He had a feeling that Lily would have added another layer if she would have known they would be eating alone together. It was clear that she wasn't immune to him, that she felt the attraction, too. Also clear that she was equally determined to fight it.

"Well, I guess technically if we eat together it's a business dinner."

"This isn't a business dinner," he said.

Her dark eyes were severe, her mouth pressed into a line. "If we were at a restaurant, I promise you I would save the receipt and write it off."

His body stirred, responding to the blatant challenge she was laying down. She wanted him, and she was determined to fight against it. He ached to release her hair from its tight confines again, to feel her lush, generous curves beneath his hands, to undo all of those little buttons, to undo her completely.

It was the wrong thing to want. But the temptation she represented was one he was finding harder and harder to resist. He didn't even want to resist it anymore.

"Sit down, Lily."

She shot him a deadly glare but settled down on the

low couch. He went into the kitchen and rummaged until he found two wineglasses and a bottle of Pinot Gris.

She took the glass, without comment, and allowed him to pour her a generous portion. A few moments later a woman from housekeeping knocked and came in with trays, setting them on the coffee table before exiting quietly.

There was a wide variety of fish, rice and noodle dishes and for a while they ate in silence. Another shock, since it was a rare thing for Lily to be silent. She always had a smart remark for every situation, and she never spared anyone her lightning-fast wit. It was one of the things he enjoyed about her.

But despite the fact that she usually filled the silence, he'd had very few real conversations with her. They kept it to work. Which was how he liked it. He'd been surprised when she'd shared about why she lived by the ocean, and felt put out when it became clear that she regretted sharing.

And it shouldn't have. It shouldn't matter. It shouldn't matter whether or not she lived by the ocean because she was a champion surfer, or if it was because she felt trapped in her home state. And yet, it had mattered.

It was easy to look at Lily and see her as a two-dimensional person. Almost an accessory to his work life, something he took inventory of. Mobile phone, laptop, Lily. And he was certain she saw him the same way sometimes. Neither of them had ever gone out of their way to connect, to know each other. He didn't see the point. When he was at work, he was at work. When he was with a woman, it was for a good time. Only Maddy and his close friends really knew much of anything about him. Even the press was ignorant of the fine details of his life. As he preferred it. If he had to live publicly he wanted to keep some aspects of his life to himself.

Now there seemed to be a shift happening in his and Lily's relationship.

It's because you want to see her naked.

That was all it was. Sex clouded a man's judgment, and while he generally thought of himself as being above that, given his amount of experience, Lily seemed to revert him back to his teenage years. Which was extremely exciting in some ways, and something part of him—the part that was below his belt, he imagined—wanted very much to explore. While another part of him, likely his brain, was telling him to ignore it.

"Have you spoken to Maddy?" Lily asked, looking at him over the rim of her wineglass as she took a sip, leaving the imprint of her glossy lipstick behind. Normally he wouldn't think anything about such a normal occurrence, but something about it, about the lingering imprint of Lily's lips, was sexy beyond reason.

"I talked to her while you were showering. She's having fun in Switzerland. No media and good skiing."

"I'm sorry she's going through this. It isn't fair. Seems to be the natural state of sexual politics though. If a woman has sex with a man, he uses it against her. If she turns him down…he still finds a way to use it against her."

"You're not the biggest fan of men, are you?"

"I like men that I know personally. Men as a species I sometimes have issues with. Or maybe, more specifically, cultural traditions that allow them to get away with pretty despicable things that women would never be forgiven for."

"Do you speak from experience?"

She slid her hand up and down the stem of the glass, the movement so erotic he felt the impact of it down in his groin. Ironic and inappropriate considering the topic of conversation. But then, he was a man. And she was very much a woman.

"Not anything close to what Maddy is dealing with, but I know what it's like for men to make assumptions."

"Jeff Campbell was making assumptions, wasn't he?"

She nodded. "Yes, he was. And I was partly glad to cancel the contract because of that. I didn't want to have to deal with another awkward conversation where I have to explain that a friendly greeting is simply a friendly greeting and not an invitation for sex."

"You called me sexist for basically saying the same thing about women I've worked with."

She frowned. "Well, you didn't have any lingering repercussions for turning your PA down."

He quirked an eyebrow. "You don't think her showing up naked in my office was over the top? What if the roles were reversed?"

She grimaced. "Okay. Point taken. People can be awful. Both genders. But I am sorry that Maddy's having to deal with this."

"Me, too. She's been through enough." He didn't usually talk about their growing-up years, or, more specifically, Maddy's growing-up years. But it seemed fair that Lily understand since she was in the middle of everything.

"She moved in with me when she was ten," he said. "My parents weren't caring for her. Not properly. So I went and got her and brought her home with me. She stayed until she went to college four years ago."

"You raised her?"

He shrugged. "More or less. I was twenty-five, no-where near ready to be a father, especially not to my ten-year-old sister, but it was what she needed. And I know I wasn't really a great substitute for a father. But I did what I could. I made sure she went to prom. And that her date—skinny kid, very annoying—got threatened within an inch of his life beforehand. A shocking number of high school students lose their virginity at prom."

It was strange to hear Gage talking like this. Like a concerned parent. Like a man who had faced things she hadn't even tried to imagine dealing with.

Lily's heart clenched tight. She'd always assumed that Gage was just a carefree playboy. The kind of man who played around simply because he had money and power and no woman would say no, and no one would look down on him for simply doing what men did.

But, just like that wildlife preserve he hadn't yet shared with the public, there was more to him. He'd raised a child. He'd been there for his sister when no one else had.

"For the record, she was back at ten o'clock on prom night," he added.

"Does that mean you let her date live?"

"I did. But I wouldn't have if he'd done anything to hurt her. Or if he'd taken advantage of her, or caused her pain in any way."

She bit her lip. "Are you going to let Callahan live?"

"Weighing the pros and cons of it."

"I didn't realize that you'd been through that with her."

He shrugged again, like he always did when things

turned personal. "I did what I had to. I wanted to do it. I love Maddy."

"It really makes sense to me now, why you're doing this, why it's so important for you to protect her. In a lot of ways you're more like a parent than a brother."

And again, she felt something shifting inside of her, felt some of her defenses weaken, begin to crumble. If he was nothing more than a carefree playboy, then it was easy to brush off her attraction to him. And while, clearly, he had strong playboy elements, he was also a good person. She liked Gage, she always had, but now she liked him more, and that complicated things, especially when the liking mixed with her steadily growing attraction for him.

She took another fortifying sip of wine and then realized that fortifying herself with the heat-inducing, slightly drugging liquid wasn't the best idea.

"I'm tired. Jet lag," she said. And lines were becoming muddled, thanks to the wine and the sudden revelation about Gage. "I should go to bed."

Gage nodded. "Good night, Lily."

Later, when she was in her bed, trying to fall asleep, she kept hearing that deep husky voice over and over again, telling her good night. And it was far too easy to imagine he was in her bed saying it, holding her close to his hard, hot body.

She wrapped herself tightly in her blanket and curled her knees up to her chest, trying to stop the ache that was pounding inside of her. The ache that was turning into a shocking feeling of emptiness that her body seemed to think only Gage could fill.

CHAPTER SIX

BREAKFAST with the board was an event. They were businessmen, so they weren't seeking public displays of affection at least, but they did want to know how the scandal with Maddy was going to affect the bottom line.

"Not at all," Lily insisted. "The incident with Maddy barely made a dent in the international media. William Callahan isn't famous worldwide. And we're going to make sure we publicize the Forrester Wildlife Preserve that Gage established here on Koh Samui."

"The cynical might argue that I set aside all of that land to keep my competition out," Gage said when the members of the board had left the table, off to a golf game Gage had arranged for them.

"Yes, the cynical might," she said. "But your motives aren't important."

"Do you really believe that?"

"In this context, yes, I do. As far as life application goes, of course motivation matters. But this is for a sound bite, a press release. They can speculate about your motives all they like, but the important thing is that you did it. At least that's how those concerned about environmental impact will see it."

"Interested in sightseeing today?"

She raised her eyebrows. "Don't we have paperwork to file, or something?"

"Not today. I thought you might enjoy seeing some of the island. The main focus of this resort is simply bringing people into the natural beauty of Thailand. That's why, at my resort, I haven't made a golf course and built bars along the beach. It would be good PR if you were familiar with the place."

She sighed. "Using my job title against me. Shameless."

He looked at her. "I can be."

Silence, the thick tense kind, settled between them again. Lily licked her suddenly dry lips, and his eyes dropped, following the movement. A rush of pure feminine pride raced through her. That she could affect a man like Gage was nothing short of incredible. She had no experience at all and he had likely slept his way through the phone book.

But she wasn't imagining it. He was feeling it too. The insistent beat pounding inside of her, demanding satisfaction.

She looked away and tried to steady her breathing, tried to think logically. They were adults, and that meant there was only one place an attraction like this would end if it was acted on. And that was in bed. All fine for most people, but she had less experience than most teenagers, and Gage was a thirty-seven-year-old man with years of experience. It was an incongruous, insane combination.

"Bring a swimsuit," he said finally, breaking the tension between them. Most of it anyway.

"I don't have one."

He frowned. "You didn't bring a swimsuit to an island?"

"It's a business trip."

He lowered his voice, his blue eyes intense. "I think it's a little more than that."

She shook her head. "No. Don't say that. Don't talk about it."

"Because if we don't talk about it we don't feel it?"

"Because it's stupid. We work together." She didn't even pretend to be ignorant of what he meant. What would the point of that be?

No matter how much she wanted to deny it there was an attraction between them. An attraction that, if she was honest, had been there, smoldering since that very first interview, the one that had not resulted in her being hired. Which was why, even though she'd been put out that he'd chosen someone else, she'd been relieved that she wouldn't be the one who had to work with him every day. Because he'd affected her in ways no other man had, and it wasn't something she'd been prepared to deal with. She still wasn't, she just didn't have a choice now, since she was stuck in a foreign country with the man, pretending to be his fiancée.

"I don't swim, actually," she said, the thought of being that exposed making her feel jittery. It was less a matter of revealing her body, and more a matter of losing her image, her business suits and killer shoes, which always helped her amp up her confidence.

He arched an eyebrow. "You don't know how to swim or you don't swim?"

"Is there a difference?"

"A pretty big one. The difference between whether or not I have to jump in and save you if you fall overboard."

She narrowed her eyes. "Okay, I know how, I just

don't." Not in front of him anyway. "And anyway, if I fell overboard, you know you would jump in after me."

A slow smile spread across his face. "Maybe. I'll have a member of the staff track down a swimsuit for you. You'll enjoy yourself. Trust me."

The boat ride out to the small island just off the south side of Koh Samui was incredible. The water was completely clear, the depths of the ocean clearly visible as they floated over the surface of the water.

Lily found herself relaxing, even in Gage's presence, which was a strange feeling. But the scenery was so gorgeous and the small yacht skimmed so smoothly over the small waves, that it was simply impossible to fight the effects.

Even the swimsuit, a barely there bikini held together with tiny strings, no longer had her feeling so tense. Of course, she was covered with a T-shirt and shorts, so that helped.

She'd worn a bikini once before. Something she'd purchased herself for her sixteenth birthday. Her mother's boyfriend had seemed to think it was some sort of invitation. She felt incredibly lucky to this day that he'd been more of a jerk, rather than being outright evil. At least he'd listened when she'd said a very emphatic no. But the lingering memory of his alcohol-flavored kiss was more than enough to remind her of where men sometimes saw invitation and opportunity.

She didn't really believe Gage would do anything like that, though. She never had. He would never need to force himself on a woman. He wouldn't anyway. She was confident in that. But the bikini itself wasn't the biggest worry. Without her business clothes, without that reinforcing barrier between them, she was afraid she might forget why she couldn't give in to the attraction they both very clearly felt.

So don't forget.

Gage steered the yacht into an alcove that was surrounded by a sheer rock face that created a natural wall of privacy around what looked like a small swimming area. The water was clear here, too. Lily could see silver flashes beneath the surface that she knew were fish.

"I can definitely see why you built a resort out here," she said.

"I visited Thailand for the first time when I was in college. I knew I wanted to do something here then. I was just waiting for the right time."

She sat up in the deck chair she'd been lounging on. "You built the business up by yourself?"

He nodded. "Started small, with residential homes that I fixed up. Then I found some land to subdivide and built a neighborhood, which got me off to a pretty good start. I started looking for investors after that."

"Why resort properties then?"

"Because they're more profitable. The industry is more stable. There's a class of people that will always vacation no matter what."

It sounded like her own reasoning for her job. It wasn't as though she loved public relations more than anything. But she was good at it, and she made good money at it. It served her sense of ambition, her drive to succeed. Her need to put more and more distance between the new Lily and the Lily she'd left in Kansas.

"How about you, Lily? Did you start your business by yourself?"

She nodded. "Yes."

"No help?"

She laughed. "No one in my family would have known how to help. Actually, I don't have all that much family. Just my mother and whatever man she's shacked up with at any given moment."

More than she'd intended to share. How did he do that? He had a way of making her want to bare all to him. Wanting to make him understand her, when she really should care.

"It takes a lot of drive to make your own success," he said, looking at the island in front of them instead of at her.

"Yes, it does. Why didn't your family help you, Gage? Your parents had money."

"I wouldn't take money from them. Not after what they did to Maddy."

The glint of rage in his eyes was so intense, so feral, that if it had been directed at her, she almost would have been frightened of him. There was so much more to Gage than she'd originally assumed. Carefree playboy. Was that really how she'd seen him just a week ago? Oh, she'd always sensed a level of intensity beneath the surface, but she'd thought that was just ambition, drive for his career. It was more. A lot more.

"At least she had you," she said softly.

There hadn't been anyone for her. Her mother had been too caught up in the soap opera of her life, and there certainly hadn't been an ally available in the scores of men her mother had lived with over the years.

A flash of a feeling, a strange longing, shook her. What would it be like to have someone support her? Stand by her no matter what? To have someone in her life that cared about her in the sacrificial way that Gage loved Maddy.

She blinked. There wasn't anyone. And she didn't

need there to be anyway. That was what made her mother so weak. Her mother needed someone else to make her feel complete, needed drama and loud fights and passionate sex to feel alive. Lily made herself feel alive. She pushed herself, supported herself. She was the only one she counted on for anything, and that was the way it had to be. If she let herself down, there was no one else to blame, and there was no one else hurt. It all came down to her.

Usually, those thoughts left her feeling fortified, but not now. It just made her feel lonely. She used to ache like this all of the time. Wish that someone would care for her, care about her. She'd let it go so long ago she hadn't realized that those old longings still existed... they were buried, but still there.

She inhaled a sharp breath of the hot, damp air.

"Of course she had me," Gage said, his voice hard. "I would never leave her to fend for herself."

A tightening sensation curled in her stomach. Envy, she realized. Envy that Maddy had someone who cared for her so much, to love her so much, even if her parents hadn't. Lily hadn't had anyone. She still didn't.

"Let's swim," she said, the words leaving her mouth before she had a chance to process them. She didn't really want to reveal her body to Gage. She valued her image, the shield she'd put up around herself, too much to make herself so exposed. But she realized that if she didn't do something she was in danger of doing something much stupider than that.

"I didn't think you swam."

"It's too beautiful to resist."

Gage dropped anchor on the boat and stepped back down on to the deck, gripping the bottom of his T-shirt and pulling it off in one fluid movement.

Lily felt her jaw go slack, and she knew that she looked as awestruck as she felt. She'd never seen Gage without a shirt. She'd mostly seen him in business attire, which was a massive treat for the eyes. And then, in preparation for the yacht trip, when he'd changed from his suit into pair of well-worn, well-fitted jeans and a threadbare T-shirt that revealed hints of his musculature beneath the soft, thin fabric, she'd found him incredible.

But now, standing in front of her with nothing but those jeans, low-slung, revealing lines that seemed to point straight down to a part of his body that should be completely off-limits to her, even in her mind, he had the power to stun her completely.

His chest was essentially mind-numbing. Acres of golden skin with just a slight dusting of dark hair, his muscles well-defined, shifting and bunching as he moved around the yacht, tying off ropes and making sure everything was secure for them to disembark.

When he straightened she couldn't help but watch the play of his ab muscles, shifting, rippling.

Oh, my...

Her heart thundered and her mouth went completely dry.

She owned beachfront property. She saw half-naked men every day of the week. And she even liked looking at them. But never, ever, had she been unable to do anything but stare. But she couldn't tear her eyes away from him.

Now she really needed a swim. And she hoped the water was cold enough to jar her out of whatever stupor her hormones were lulling her into.

He unsnapped the top button of his jeans and the

intensely provocative motion shook her back to reality. "What are you doing?"

He didn't say anything, only gave her a wicked grin and lowered the zipper on his pants, shrugging them down his slim hips, revealing his swim shorts.

She narrowed her eyes and grabbed the hem of her T-shirt before hauling it over her head. She tugged her shorts down and tossed them onto the chair before the full impact of what she'd done and what she was wearing could hit her.

His eyes raked over her, his expression mirroring everything she was feeling, although he didn't have the dumbfounded look she was sure had been etched onto her face. No, there was nothing confusing about any of this for him. His expression showed nothing but intent. He knew what he wanted, and he knew what to do about it, and suddenly she felt as if she would trade anything, even half of her kingdom so to speak, for an ounce of that surety. To feel confident. To know she could have what she wanted and suffer nothing for the indulgence.

Her self-imposed strictures had never bothered her before. She'd been happy simply putting her head down and working, climbing the ladder, doing everything she could to put miles between herself and her past.

Now, for the first time, she wondered if she'd missed something somewhere along the way.

Part of her wanted to give him the disclaimer that she never wore such revealing swimwear. But another part of her, the more stubborn part, didn't want him to know that she felt totally out of her depth being alone with a man in the middle of a tropical paradise, wearing little more than a few strings tied together and passed off as swimwear.

Instead she reached up and released her hair from its clip, letting it fall down over her shoulders in a wave before she headed over to the ladder that led to the water below them.

She could feel him watching her, could feel the heat of his gaze, touching her like a caress. A shiver ran through her. Her breasts felt heavy and she knew, without having to look down, that her hardened nipples were clearly visible through the thin fabric of her bikini.

She turned and put her foot on the first rung of the ladder, very determinedly not looking at Gage. She made it halfway down the ladder when Gage dove over the side of the boat, his perfect entry barely making a ripple in the clear pool of water.

She rolled her eyes and continued down the ladder. "I'm very impressed," she quipped when he came back to the surface.

"I am, too," he said, not bothering to hide his frank appraisal of her.

Embarrassment warred with pride and arousal. It was the strangest thing. Men had liked her looks before. Men—adult men—had been making passes at her since she was a freshman in high school. Her first, immediate response had always been to discourage. It always made her feel defensive.

But this didn't feel like something she was being subjected to. She felt a part of it, like they were both trapped in the same swirling undertow, unable to escape the pull. She felt like she knew Gage's thoughts, knew them and shared them. That their desire mirrored each others.

She dropped into the water, shocked at how warm it was. Gage swam to her, and put his hand over hers, over where she was still clinging to the metal ladder.

"You can swim, right?"

She nodded. "I just haven't in a long time."

His touch was doing all kinds of things to her, making her ache, making her want, but also, offering comfort. It wasn't like anything she'd ever felt before, and she hated that she was feeling it for him. That she was feeling it for her boss.

He smoothed his thumb over her ring finger, over the ring that was settled there. His ring. "Don't lose this. I don't want to have to send a dive team out."

She looked at her hand. "Oh!" She hadn't even realized the ring was still there. And it had felt so heavy at first that she'd been conscious of it all the time. She didn't even want to know what that might mean. "I can go put it back."

"I've got it."

He took her hand from the ladder and slid the ring off of her finger, climbing quickly back onto the boat.

She flexed her fingers. Now they felt bare. It was an irony she didn't enjoy.

Gage came back down the ladder and she moved to the side as he slid back into the water beside her. "Can you swim to the shore?"

She nodded with more confidence than she felt.

"Let's see if you can beat me," he said.

She couldn't fight the slight smile that tugged at the corner of her mouth. "You know me so well. How can I resist a challenge?"

"I knew you couldn't."

He turned and swam toward shore, smooth strokes barely making a splash in the crystal water. She followed, trying hard to keep up, but she couldn't. He must have known she couldn't or he wouldn't have issued the challenge. He probably swam competitively or something.

She gave up trying to preserve her makeup and slipped under the water, knowing she would be faster that way. When she finally surfaced to get air, Gage was already on shore, lying on the beach, the white sand a light dusting on his golden skin.

When she finally got to where her feet could touch bottom she walked the rest of the way onto the warm sand. "That was cruel," she said, wiping water, and what she was certain would be trails of black mascara, from beneath her eyes.

"You should always carefully consider challenges."

"I accept every challenge."

"Which is why you lose some of them."

She scowled at him and sat next to him, the heat from the sand burning her partially exposed backside.

Gage was having trouble drawing breath, but it had nothing do to with his recent physical exertion, and everything to do with the woman sitting next to him. He'd seen Lily polished to perfection, ready to tackle the press. He'd seen her dressed for an art gala, her hair and gown perfectly pressed. But he'd never seen her like this.

Her brown hair hung wet and curling, her makeup washed off by the saltwater. He could see a light sprinkling of freckles over her nose and across her high cheekbones. She looked softer, more touchable.

And then there was her body. A body that had inspired him to get into the water as quickly as possible so he could avoid revealing to her the effect she was having on him.

Her curves were always flattered by whatever she

wore, but seeing them revealed by the bright red bikini
was an entirely different experience.

Her pale breasts, high and firm, her nipples puckered and tight against the wet, clinging fabric of her
top, her long, exposed legs, more perfect than his mind
could have ever imagined them to be, had him hard and
aching. He wanted her, and all of the reasons for him not
to have her were becoming less and less significant.

She leaned back, took a deep breath, her breasts
rising and falling, his eyes drawn to the pale, creamy
skin. "I should take vacations. Or go outside of my
condo and go the beach once in a while. You make time
for recreation and you're a lot more successful than I
am."

"I lived eight years with very little personal life. I've
learned to make the time," he said.

"I need to, I think. I didn't before we came here,
but…now I do."

She rolled to her side, propping her head up on her
elbow. His heart leapt. There wasn't a single swimsuit
model that could possibly be more beautiful than Lily,
with her unconscious, uncalculated sensuality. It was a
provocative pose, her breasts nearly spilling out of her
top, her waist seeming even smaller, her hip rounder, in
that position, yet he could see nothing in her eyes that
even hinted at any knowledge of it.

Lily wasn't sheltered. She wasn't naive. But she
seemed so unaware of the power she could wield over
a man. Of the power she had over him now.

"I think I… My life is so focused on work. On getting further and further ahead. I never even give myself
a chance to enjoy anything else in life. I love my job,
and I enjoy work, but…I never date."

"I find that hard to believe."

"Okay, I've dated," she said. "In fact, recently I've had several very disastrous dates set up by well-meaning friends."

"Why would you have your friends set you up? Why not just date someone you meet and are attracted to?"

She laughed softly. "That would require getting out of my house or the office on occasion."

"You could have any man you wanted," he said, his voice rough.

She looked at him, her dark eyes unveiled for a moment, the heat in their dark depths calling out to him, making his body ache for her. Making him ache for her in more than just physical ways. "I haven't really wanted any men."

"You want me," he said, not seeing any point in skirting the issue.

"I...sometimes I think I do," she said, her voice a whisper. She looked away from him then. It was strange, seeing her unsure, seeing her vulnerable. He wanted her to be bold, to show confidence, to give him some kind of sign that she was open to a purely physical fling.

If her take-no-prisoners attitude from the boardroom carried over to the bedroom, she would. But when it came to attraction she seemed to lose all of the boldness. All that hardened attitude turned soft. It made him want to comfort her. To just hold her against him until the tension left her body and she softened against him, softened for him.

He sucked in a breath, consigning the consequences of his actions to hell, and leaned in, brushing his lips against hers. He waited, waited to see what her reaction would be. That wasn't his usual style, but she was nothing like his usual women.

She looked at him then, her dark eyes unsure. He

kissed her again, more insistently this time, his hands
skimming the dip of her waist, the curve of her hip.
When he slid his hands around to her backside and
slipped his fingers just barely beneath the waistband of
her bikini bottoms she sucked in a shocked breath, parting her lips, giving him the chance to slide his tongue
into her mouth.

She brought her hands up to his arms and gripped
his biceps, clinging to him. She moaned softly as he
abandoned her mouth, pressing kisses to the soft, tender
column of her throat. Kissing the pulse that fluttered at
the base of her neck.

Then he captured her mouth again, moving both of
his hands to her backside and bringing her so that she
was resting partly on top of him. Her thigh was pressed
against his erection, the slight pressure pleasure and
torture at the same time.

She pulled away, her eyes wide, her breathing harsh.
"Oh…" She rested her head on his chest, her heart
pounding hard enough that he could feel it against his
stomach. "How do you do that?"

He chuckled, despite the persistent ache in his groin
reminding him they were nowhere near finished, and
ran his fingers through her hair. "Do what?"

"You make me forget why this is a very bad idea.
You make me forget why I decided it can't happen. I
can't think of anything when you kiss me."

"That's a good thing, Lily."

"I don't know that it is."

Lily slithered away from Gage and stood on wobbly
legs. She felt light-headed, like she might pass out. She'd
never, ever, been kissed like that. Oh, she'd been kissed,
she'd been pretty thoroughly kissed in fact, but it had
never felt anything like that. It had never made her

forget where she was, who she was, why she shouldn't be kissing him.

Usually, when she was being kissed, she was wondering if the guy was going to ask to come in for a cup of "coffee," and how she was going to turn him down. But she had a feeling Gage could have stripped off her insubstantial swimsuit and she never would have noticed, or been upset about it. In fact, she had a feeling she simply would have embraced it, the mind-numbing pleasure of his touch, and gone after something they would likely both regret later.

She sucked in a sharp breath. "We've already been over the fact that neither of us does the serious thing," she said slowly. "Which means…which means if we were to have sex it would be a fling. An affair."

He stood up, too, his arousal still blatantly pressing against the front of his shorts. She tried, valiantly, not to look, but failed. She'd never seen such an aggressively male sight in her life. And he was tempting her all over again.

She didn't need tempting. She needed a moment of sanity.

Gage nodded. "That's how I conduct my relationships, Lily."

She looked at the water, at the waves lapping against the shore. "What about my job?"

"Your job isn't in jeopardy either way."

"Then I guess the only question is whether or not *I* can do a fling."

"You think you might want more?" he asked.

"No. I don't want more, I know that. I like my life as it is. But then…" She'd seen her mother on the brink of insanity over men, crying when they didn't call, crying when they did. Throwing things when they cheated, screaming when they broke up with her.

Lily had worked so hard to never be that person. She'd avoided relationships, avoided any kind of deep, emotional involvement. Part of her was afraid that, while she knew she didn't want to enter into relationship hell, she would forget that as soon as she crossed that line with a man.

Sex seemed to have some sort of strange power over women, a power than went beyond the simple pleasure it provided. She didn't want to be subject to that.

"You're concerned it would be awkward working together?"

"Yes." *Among other things.* "And my job is very important to me. I don't think it's worth compromising that for a fling."

He moved to her, cupping her cheek, stroking her skin with his thumb. "It would be a very good fling."

She closed her eyes, fighting the rising tide of heat and trying to lay claim on her own body again. "I'm sure of that."

Fear warred with common sense and desire. She wanted him, but she was afraid. Afraid of who this desire might make her become. Afraid of losing control. Of giving any of her hard-won control to him, both in the bedroom and in her life in general.

She hadn't been worried about that when he'd been kissing her though. She hadn't been able to worry about anything.

She felt like she was standing on the edge of one of the rocky cliffs that surrounded the island, poised to jump into the water, unsure of how deep it would be. She could turn and walk away, and never know, but everything would be back to normal, back to her life as she knew it, as she had made it to be. Or she could jump, not knowing what would happen, not knowing if she would survive.

"I…I can't." It was too much. He made her feel too much.

She saw a flash of frustration in his blue eyes, but it didn't linger. He cupped her face with both hands now, his touch tender. "If you change your mind, you can always come to me," he said, his voice strained. "But you will have to come to me. I don't force my attentions on women who don't want them. I have no need to."

He turned from her and waded back into the water, swimming back to the yacht.

A feeling of sadness washed over her. She almost wished he would have promised to seduce her. Now that it was up to her she knew she would never find the courage. And she hated that. Hated that she still lived with so much weakness. Weakness she'd been able to ignore, been able to deny, until she'd met Gage. Weakness she was still too afraid to try and overcome.

CHAPTER SEVEN

LILY disappeared into her room when they arrived back at the vacation home and reappeared a few hours later, her armor back in place. Her hair was pinned perfectly into place again, her makeup covering her freckles.

"Any plans for tonight?" she asked, her high heels clicking on the wooden floor as she moved across the room, keeping her distance from him as she settled onto the low couch.

"We're treating the board to a traditional dinner on the beach. Complete with traditional dancing."

"I love that idea. Will you be doing it for regular guests, too?"

He nodded. "Yes. When I first visited Thailand I was backpacking with friends, no luxury resorts or anything. We ate in the marketplaces and avoided the tourist traps. I want to bring that element into the resort. Luxury, but with a chance to experience the culture."

She shot him a severe look, her lush lips pulled into a tight line. "We're putting that in the press release when the resort opens. I don't understand why you're so reluctant to give the public some information about the good things that you do."

He let out an exasperated sigh. "As you said, Lily, they call it a private life for a reason. I don't see the point in sharing every aspect of myself with the press. I don't talk about the fact that I raised Maddy because I'm afraid it would embarrass her. She feels like she must have been unlovable for our parents to neglect her like they did, and I'm not about to let the public know the circumstances of her life. It isn't fair to her."

"And the other things? The sanctuary? Your respect for the Thai culture?"

"Personal."

"But it's not really. It relates back to your business, to your image. And really, why not let people know you're actually a decent person?"

He laughed. "My parents made so many charitable contributions they were hailed as the most generous couple in the San Diego area. They have plaques on schools and hospitals. It didn't make them good people."

Gage knew, better than most, that public image and private image were not the same thing. His parents were the most self-absorbed, selfish people he'd ever encountered, and that included every one of his past mistresses.

All of the flash, all of the grand gestures, meant very little when the only thing behind it was a desire for more publicity. His parents didn't care about anyone, or anything, beyond their own ambitions. He'd worked all of his young adult years to establish his business. He'd been so determined to impress them with who he'd become.

He'd made his first million, his first two million, and still he'd waited. Finally he'd stopped caring. Probably on the day Maddy called, telling him she hadn't eaten for three days, not because his parents were too poor to provide her with food, but because they were so busy living their very important lives they'd forgotten their daughter. That was also the day he'd brought his sister to live with him.

"The fact that my parents were willing to spare the time to write a check to boost their likability, to gain more business, didn't make them good, or giving, or caring," he growled, rage coursing through him at the memory. "I don't play that game."

He didn't know what it was about Lily that made him say those kinds of things. She made him want to explain. If it were any other woman, any other employee, he simply would have let them think what they wanted, no explanation offered. But she wasn't just another woman, and she wasn't just an employee, either. He wasn't certain how he felt about her falling outside of those clear, distinct categories.

"I understand that. I understand how much parents can motivate what you do and don't do." She looked up, meeting his gaze for the first time since they'd kissed on the beach. "My mother...growing up with her was difficult. Her relationships and all the drama they came with were the most important things to her. They consumed her and I hated it. I hated seeing her so controlled by this twisted emotion that she called love that made her do and accept the most horrible things."

"That's why you don't do relationships."

She nodded in confirmation. "That's why I don't do relationships. Ever. I don't want to turn into that. I don't want anyone or anything controlling me like that."

"I wouldn't, Lily, you know that. I don't do the toxic relationship thing. Women I date are free to be their own people. I'm not looking to force anyone to fit into my lifestyle, because I'm not looking to add anyone to my life permanently."

Lily bit her bottom lip until it hurt. She was tempted, again, so very tempted, to take Gage up on his offer. She'd come out of the bedroom with the best of intentions, her protective shield in place, ready and willing to resist him and carry on like she always had. But that was impossible. She *knew* now. She knew about the power of desire.

Wanting sexual satisfaction was entirely different than wanting another person. It wasn't simply about wanting to reach the peak of pleasure, it was about wanting to touch him, taste him, explore him. It wasn't about just wanting a man. That would have been much easier to cope with. This was about wanting one man specifically. She wanted Gage. No one else.

But the fear wasn't gone. Being with him was complicated, and not just because he was her boss. Sleeping with him would mean no barriers. There would be no way for her to stay in control the whole time. She knew that just from one kiss. Ironic since she'd always thought that when she did choose to have sex with a man her problem would be forcing herself to give up her control.

She'd imagined she would find it impossible to reach orgasm because she would be too concerned about being vulnerable, out of control. She hadn't anticipated the man being able to rob her of it as neatly and quickly as Gage was able to.

When he was touching her, she *wanted* to surrender, wanted to simply allow him to sweep her off her feet and take her on the journey her body was begging to go on. And that was frightening.

She closed her eyes and swallowed hard. "Give me until after the dinner tonight," she said. "I'll decide by then."

Gage's expression didn't change, his firm jaw set, his eyes unreadable. "Decide?"

"Whether or not I'm ready for a fling," she said then added, "a fling with you."

"I didn't imagine you meant with one of our distinguished members of the board," he said, his voice husky.

She laughed shakily. "I wanted to make sure. I know how people can spin things. I work with the media, remember?"

He leaned in, so close she could feel his breath fanning over her cheek. She closed her eyes as a shiver slithered through her body, starting in her shoulders and spreading everywhere, leaving her nipples tight and aching, her body wet with wanting him.

"This isn't really your thing, is it? You're not a fling kind of girl."

Her eyes fluttered open, reality crowding all the lovely arousal that had been making her feel warm and languid and brave. "You don't think so?"

Of course she wasn't. She was a twenty-seven-year-old virgin, but that admission wasn't about to escape her lips. She didn't want him thinking he was special, or that there was something wrong with her, or that she was suddenly going to start salivating whenever she saw a diamond ring. This wasn't emotional for her, not really, this was about physical need.

She trusted Gage, in a certain respect, but that was the only emotion involved. Still she'd had the opportunity to observe how Gage was in relationships. He wasn't controlling, or manipulative. He was honest about what he wanted and both parties in the relationship ended up satisfied in more ways than one. That was what she wanted, all she wanted.

And she had to do this. She had to take control of her life, her body, her sexuality. Now that she realized how much of her life had been controlled by her mother's actions, now that she saw just how much power she gave to the many men that had paraded through her mother's life, to the drama and the fights and the tears, she knew she had to move beyond it. This was her chance. If she was brave enough to take it.

"I haven't had time to have one since coming to work for you." The honest truth, even if it was misleading.

"Just don't forget that it's only a fling. Women can be emotional about sex and if it's been a while for you…"

She met his gaze, her heart pounding hard. "Gage, have I ever seemed like the kind of person who doesn't know her own mind? Let me worry about it. I promise you, I don't have one single repressed fantasy about love and happily ever after anywhere inside of me. I'm far too practical." She stood from the couch, trying to keep her expression cool, trying to ignore her rapidly beating pulse. "And anyway, it's only a fling. I'll probably forget about it in a few years' time."

Gage crossed the room, his expression intense. He bent down and hooked his arm around her waist, bringing her into a standing position, hauling her up against him. "You won't forget me, Lily," he said, his voice rough.

He leaned down, his mouth urgent on hers. There was nothing slow about this kiss, nothing like the kiss they'd shared on the beach. This was fire and urgency. This wasn't a slow tasting, this was a feast. She parted her lips for him, meeting his tongue thrust for thrust, lacing her fingers through his short dark hair, pulling him even harder against her.

His big hand cupped her bottom, bringing her tightly against his body, letting her feel the hard ridge of his erection pressing against her stomach.

He pulled away from her suddenly, his breathing harsh, his chest rising and falling. When he withdrew completely and stepped away from her she was afraid she might melt to the floor without his arms to support her.

She put a hand on her lips, feeling how hot and swollen they were.

"After the dinner, tell me what you want," he said gruffly. "Be very sure."

"I know what I want now," she said with a boldness she didn't feel. "Do you want me? I mean *me*, not just sex." She didn't know why, but that seemed important. She didn't want him picturing one of his little blonde heiresses while he was in bed with her. That was a matter of pride.

He took hold of her wrist and pressed her hand against his chest, against his raging heartbeat. "Does that feel like I want you?"

"Yes," she whispered. She looked down and saw, very clearly, the outline of his rigid erection pressing against his jeans. She swallowed. There was no room for her to be timid. He wouldn't want a shy little virgin in his bed, that much was obvious from the type of women he chose to date. Which meant she'd have to be a confident virgin, a virgin who could fake more experience than she had. Well, experience she might not have, but she had desire.

She slid her hand down his chest, moved her palm to cover the hard ridge of his arousal. He let his head fall back, his breath hissing between his teeth. "So does this," she said.

"Careful," he groaned. "Or neither of us will be making it to dinner."

A sliver of pleasure wound its way through her, along with a surge of adrenaline. This was a new kind of power, power she hadn't anticipated. She'd assumed, because of the way her mother behaved, that when it came to sex, men held all the cards. But she knew now that wasn't true. Right now, holding him in her hand, she was in control. She was the one driving him crazy with desire, pushing him beyond his control.

"Well, we can't have that. I'm really looking forward to dinner."

He leaned in, pressed a kiss to her neck, to where her pulse was fluttering rapidly. "I'm looking forward to dessert."

The flickering light from the bonfire, the lingering heat from the day, combined with the slow, seductive music, made Lily feel like she was under a spell. Maybe she was, because she had no idea what sort of magic had bewitched her into thinking she could have a no-strings relationship with Gage. But even now she wasn't afraid, not even after having time to reflect on what it would mean for her. What it might make her feel.

She wanted him. Why should her dysfunctional childhood keep her from having something she wanted? She'd never given it that sort of power in any other area of her life. In fact, she'd been determined to overcome it no matter what. But when it came to men, she'd let it hold her back.

It wasn't as though there were any missed opportunities she regretted, no men she wished she'd been able to take the chance on. But if she didn't find out what it was like with Gage, she knew she would regret that.

It would be a holiday romance. Not even a romance, it would be nothing but holiday sex. She would find out what it was like, satisfy her curiosity, satisfy the flame that burned low in her body, and move on. And so would he.

They were adults, there was no reason they couldn't be adult about it. No reason at all.

She looked at Gage, at the way the orange flames highlighted his sharp cheekbones and angular jaw. He was such a gorgeous man, and she'd kissed his perfect lips. Anticipation made her feel restless, edgy. Needy.

Soon she would know what he looked like without clothes covering his amazing body. Soon, every part of him would be hers. To explore, to touch, to taste.

"I think this is an amazing investment opportunity you have here, Mr. Forrester," one of the board members, she wasn't sure which one, said.

"It is," she said, sitting up straighter. "And what Gage is doing here goes well beyond simple tourism. He's offering a true, authentic experience, with as little or as much luxury as the guest would like to experience."

The older man gave Gage a sly smile. "Not a bad idea, Forrester, getting your PR specialist so sweetened up."

Gage scooted closer to Lily, looping his arm around her waist. "Lily has more professional integrity than anyone I've ever met. Myself included. Our relationship has nothing to do with the quality of her work. I'd recommend her business to anyone."

Lily was shocked to hear Gage give her such an emphatic endorsement, and she said as much when the members of the board were either too intoxicated to pay attention, or had gone back to their rooms.

"It's true," Gage said, shrugging. "You're great at

what you do. My attraction to you has nothing to do with how well you do your job."

"And when our relationship is over you're planning on pawning me off? Professionally speaking, I mean." She hated the insecurity in her voice, hated the slight quiver that made her sound weak. What did it matter if he was planning on letting her go? As long as her next job paid as well, it didn't matter whether she stayed with Forrestation or not. She'd done a wonderful job for his company, and there was ample evidence of that.

"Not at all. I'll have no problem working with you after things end, Lily. It's never been an issue for me. I'm still on good terms with most of the women I've had relationships with, and if I'm not, it's because of them, not me."

"After we leave Thailand, it's over," she said, with much more finality than she felt. But it was vital, absolutely necessary that she put a limit on it. That this was madness brought on by a sensual setting. Madness that did not move into the office with them.

He raised his eyebrows, his mouth quirked in a sardonic half smile. "Shall we sign a contract?"

She sniffed. "I don't think that's necessary, but I don't see the point of bringing it back into the office, either."

"You drive a hard bargain, Ms. Ford."

"I learned from the best, Mr. Forrester."

He leaned in and kissed her on the forehead, his lips warm, the feeling of comfort it brought her making a flutter of panic spring to life in her belly. He wasn't supposed to make her feel things. He pulled back and ran his hand over her smooth, neatly tied hair. "You need to wear your hair down for me. It's sexy."

She searched for some witty, off-the-cuff reply, but

she lost the ability to think when he leaned in again and kissed her, the pressure of his lips tender at first, then more urgent. She put her hand on her cheek, slid her tongue over his bottom lip. Yes, she was making the right choice. She wanted this. She wanted something beyond business, something just for herself. No one had to know. Actually, everyone would believe it had happened now, with their fake engagement making headline news, whether it happened or not. Which made it all the more tempting to indulge.

Just now the only thing she could feel was a throbbing urgency that started at the apex of her thighs and radiated out. Made her feel empty and excited all at the same time.

"I think we should go back to the room," she whispered, kissing his neck, tasting the salt of his skin.

"I think that's a very good idea."

Now that Lily was standing in Gage's room, looking at the big bed in the corner, she didn't feel as confident as she had on the beach. As she had when he was kissing her. She still wanted him, but all of her insecurities were back. She wished she had something to help boost her confidence.

Sexy lingerie would have helped. Clothes always helped her slip into her role, helped her create the image she was striving to project. She used it for work to great effect and she needed it desperately now. Needed something to help her be that confident woman that she always tried to portray in the office.

But she didn't have any lingerie. She hadn't really been expecting to have wild island sex with her boss... or anyone, for that matter.

Gage came up behind her, put his arms around her,

kissed her neck gently, letting her feel the evidence of his arousal against her back. It was very compelling evidence.

She let out a slow breath. "Turn the lights off," she said.

He spun her around so that she was facing him. "I want to be able to see you. I've fantasized about how you might look. What color your nipples are. I want to see your face when I make you come."

Heat flooded her cheeks and she knew she was blushing like the virgin she was.

"Does that bother you?" he asked, his dark brows drawn together, his expression tight.

She shook her head. "It's…it's okay. I liked hearing you talk like that." She was surprised to discover that bit of information about herself.

Yes, hearing him say things like that was embarrassing in a way, and she knew she wasn't going to be able to give him anything like it in return, but hearing him talk like that…it was enough to help her get lost, to forget who she was, who he was, and just embrace the desire that was rolling through her in waves.

"But I would feel better with the light off," she said.

He cupped her chin with his hand, ran his thumb lightly over her bottom lip. "Do you always make love with the light off?"

Make love. It was the first time he'd called it that. Maybe he thought it was too crude to call it what it was now that they were in the bedroom. Maybe that was his version of gentlemanly conduct. She wished he'd just stick to the basics and not muddle things. Not make her feel like they might be about to *make love* when she knew they were just going to have sex.

"I…" She tried to come up with something that wasn't a lie. "I prefer the lights off." There. She was being economical with the truth, but she wasn't out-and-out lying.

He came back to her kissed her gently on the lips before walking over to the other side of the room and turning the main light off. The windows were still open, casting silver moonlight over the bed, but it was better than the full glare of a sixty-watt bulb.

Her heart thundered hard when Gage walked to the bed and started to unbutton his shirt, his movements quick. Now she understood why he'd wanted the light on. She wished she could see him. But then she would lose her covering, and she wasn't prepared to deal with that.

He shrugged the shirt off and it fell to the floor. She could see the outline of his muscles, the moonlight highlighting the ridges and valleys on his body. She swallowed, her throat suddenly dry.

"Come here, Lily," he said softly.

She moved toward him, heart thundering. She was shaking, with nerves, with need, with the enormity of everything. It shouldn't be such a big deal. It was only sex. People had it every day, and then afterward, they walked away. She would do the same.

"Kiss me," she said. "Now." Because when he kissed her, everything made sense, everything seemed right.

He didn't move, he only offered her a half smile that she could see in the pale moonlight, the rest of his handsome face hidden in the shadows. "I told you, Lily, you have to come to me."

She sucked in a breath and walked toward him, putting her hands flat against his chest, his body hard and hot, so masculine. She slid her hands up to his shoulders, his coarse chest hair rough against her palms. She leaned in and kissed him on the corner of his mouth, a move she hoped would tease him, because it was teasing her.

He turned his head and captured her mouth with his, the kiss turning hungry in an instant. She wrapped her arms around his neck, pressing her breasts tightly against that hard, broad chest, the action helping to soothe the sting of her aroused nipples.

He moved his hands around to cup her breasts, to tease the hardened buds. She moaned into his mouth, the sound beyond her control, an expression of pleasure she couldn't have held back if she'd been conscious enough to try.

He wrenched his lips away from hers, pressing a hot, openmouthed kiss to the side of her neck, the touch so erotic it made her knees buckle.

"I have wanted you," he said, kissing her collar-bone, "from the first moment I saw you." He kissed the curve of her breast. "I've wanted you naked, in my bed, flushed with desire."

"Now you have me," she said, the words escaping before she could turn them over in her mind, before she could really analyze what she meant. What they might mean to him.

"Yes," he said, his blue eyes glinting, "I do."

He unbuttoned the top of her shirt then took care of the rest of the buttons with a practiced ease she was thankful for. He made it seem so easy, so smooth, that she forgot to be nervous when her shirt fell open, revealing her lacy bra.

He made quick work of that, too, both items of clothing falling to the floor. He moved his hands back to her bare breasts and teased her hardened nipples. Her head fell back, more uncontrollable sounds of pleasure coming from her mouth. All she could do was simply enjoy what he was doing to her, because she had no hope of doing anything else.

He replaced his hands with his mouth, sucking her nipple deep inside, before laving it with the flat of his tongue. "You taste as good as I imagined you would," he said.

Kneeling down in front of her, he undid the closure on her shorts and pulled them down her legs, taking her panties with them. He leaned in then, his breath hot on her just before he claimed her with his mouth, his lips and tongue working magic on her clitoris. She gripped his shoulders trying to steady herself, trying to keep from dissolving into a whimpering puddle at his feet.

Tension started building in her stomach, so tight she thought her legs might buckle. She took a breath, trying to fight the growing sensation of pleasure. She knew what it meant. She was on the brink of orgasm, her whole body trembling with the effort to hold it at bay while he continued to subject her to an onslaught of pleasure.

She threw her head back, fought the rising tide that was threatening to overtake her, threatening to drown her. He'd brought her up so high that if she went over the edge, she was afraid of what might happen. Of what she might do. Of what he might make her feel.

"Enough," she panted, desperate for respite, needing a moment to capture her sanity again.

"You don't want it like this?" he asked, standing and flicking the snap of his jeans open and shrugging them off.

She shook her head, her eyes glued to his body, what she could see of it in the dim lighting. She'd never seen

a naked man in person before. He was almost awe-
inspiring. His body so different from hers. He was so
masculine, muscular, his erection thick and tempting.
It scared her how much she wanted him. How much
she wanted to feel him inside of her. How necessary it
suddenly seemed.

She sat on the bed, her legs shaking, her whole body
shaking, inside and out.

Gage got onto the bed, leaned over her and moved his
hands behind her head, unclipping her bun and weaving
his fingers through her hair, spreading it out around
her. "I fantasized about this, seeing all of your beautiful hair fanned over my pillow. It's sexier than I could
have imagined."

Lily hadn't imagined that there would be so much
talking involved in sex, but Gage knew just how to
say the right things to make her feel like her body was
going up in flames. His words worked with his touch,
bringing her to the edge again, making her feel like she
might burn to cinders if she couldn't have him.

And this time, there was nothing she could do to stop
it. It was like her body belonged to him, like only he
could control it. Like he had to power to elicit whatever
response he wanted. She closed her eyes, shutting out
the thought. Shutting out everything but the desire that
was coursing through her.

"I want you, Gage," she said. "I need you." She slid
her hands over his back, over his tight butt. His body
was perfect, everything a man's body should be. And he
was all hers, for tonight at least, to explore and touch.
To have his body joined to hers.

He reached over to the nightstand and rummaged
for a moment before pulling out a condom packet, tearing it open and rolling the protection on in one swift

movement. Then he kissed her, parting her thighs gently and settling between them.

She loved the feeling of having him over her, of feeling his naked body pressed against every naked inch of hers.

He nudged at her damp entrance with the head of his erection and she spread her legs wider, hoping it might help her accommodate him. He put his hand underneath her backside and lifted her slightly before thrusting into her.

The flash of pain shocked her, but it was over quickly and then she just felt full. So deliciously full. Never in her life had she felt so complete, yet so needy at the same time. Having him inside of her was wholly satisfying, while also managing to create a deep need in her that she knew only he could answer.

"Lily?" His voice was rough, the tendons in his neck standing out, a testament to the strain it caused him to speak, to keep himself still.

She kissed him, and she felt his body shuddered inside of her, his shaft growing harder, increasing the feeling of fullness. Increasing her growing pleasure. "Gage, let me have you."

She knew the exact moment he lost his control. He withdrew before thrusting full back inside of her. She arched into him, the feeling so exquisite she thought she might break apart. She gripped his buttocks as he rode her, wrapped her legs around his calves as she moved against him in rhythm. Her climax started to build, the tension inside of her reaching heights she thought were impossible.

If the peak she'd nearly reached earlier had been frightening, this one was completely terrifying. All-consuming. Her entire being trembled, the need for release pulling her muscles tight, making her entire body tense. She couldn't fight it. Didn't want to fight. She needed to finish it, no matter what. There was no other choice. Her control was given over to him.

"Oh, Gage, oh, please," she breathed, not knowing quite what she needed from him.

He moved his hands to her breasts, brushed his thumbs over her nipples, the added stimulation just what she needed to push her over the edge. The dam that had been holding back the flood burst and pleasure rushed through, overtaking her. She froze, her back arched, her mouth open on a soundless scream as her body tightened around his. He thrust into her, harder, more wildly, his movements lacking any control. Then he found his release on a masculine groan of pleasure.

On the heels of her release, of the amazing burst of pleasure, came a wave of emotion so strong it made her ache. She held on to him for a while, feeling his heart beat against her chest, listening to the sound of his broken, labored breathing. Her body shook and she felt warmth on her cheeks. She put her hand up and touched her face, feeling the wetness left by her tears.

CHAPTER EIGHT

GAGE looked at Lily, flushed, satisfied and crying, tears rolling down her cheeks, little sobs making her body shiver beneath his.

"Are you hurt?" he asked, his chest tightening. He'd never been with a virgin before, but even without the experience, he was certain that Lily had been one. And it was causing a riot of emotions to roll through him, emotions he'd never dealt with in his life, and didn't want to deal with now.

"I…" She sucked in a shaking breath. "No."

He withdrew from her body and rolled over so that he was still close, but no longer connected to her. He needed at least that much space, that much of a chance to regain his sanity.

He drew her into his arms, let her cry. His muscles were so tense he felt like they might seize up. Everything in him wanted to run, but he forced himself to stay, to hold her until the tears stopped falling.

She pulled away from him, scrubbed her arm across her cheeks, leaving her face red and puffy. It was rare to see Lily look anything less than perfect, and even rarer to see her when she wasn't composed. Those moments when she'd come apart in his arms, she hadn't been composed or businesslike. And now, with her nose cherry-colored from crying and her brown hair tangled from their recent lovemaking, she was still beautiful to him. Possibly more beautiful than she'd ever been.

"I'm sorry," she said stiffly.

"Why didn't you just tell me? Didn't you think I might want to know?" he said, the clawing feeling in his stomach making his voice harsher than he'd intended.

"No, Gage, I didn't. My experience, or lack of it, is none of your business."

"I told you, this is temporary."

She turned her head sharply, dark eyes glittering. "And I told you that we're finished when we leave Thailand. Nothing has changed. I didn't tell you that I was a virgin, which is what I assume your issue is, because it was a nonissue to me. Therefore, I wouldn't think it would matter to you." She blew out a breath. "I should go to my own room. This was a mistake."

She moved to leave and he took her arm. "No. Lily, you're not leaving. You're staying with me, in my bed." And why that should matter to him, he didn't know. He wasn't the kind of guy who cuddled afterward. In fact, he usually left the hotel sometime after his lover had fallen asleep. If they didn't leave first.

But it didn't seem right to take Lily's virginity and have her sleep alone. A litany of curse words scrolled through his mind. He didn't want it to matter that he was the first man she'd been with. He didn't want her to be different in any way. She was right, it was her choice. She was a twenty-seven-year-old woman, not a young girl that he'd seduced.

"I would feel more comfortable in my own room."

"Too bad. Clause five of our fling contract says we share a bed when we make love."

"I don't remember approving that."

"And I don't remember seeing anything about you being a virgin."

"I told you, it doesn't matter."

He blew out an exasperated breath. "It does, Lily, whether you think so or not, it does. You didn't know you would cry. You didn't know how it would make you feel."

She shrugged. "It was a release. It just happened to release tears, too. I'm not going to lie, it was a fantastic orgasm." He noticed that she angled her face away when she said it. Her voice was casual, but it was obvious that she didn't feel casual.

"The last thing I want to do is hurt you, but I can't give more than I've offered."

"Honestly, Gage, I don't want more than you've offered. Why do you think I was a virgin? It wasn't because I was saving myself. It's because I didn't want the hassle."

She gathered the sheets up and moved to climb out of bed.

"Lily, stay with me. I'm not going to turn this into something that seems sordid and dirty by having you go and sleep in your own room."

She stayed still for a moment, her expression cool, her dark eyes focused on a point other than his face. But after a moment she settled back into bed, pulling the sheets up as high under her arms as she could.

He leaned in and kissed her bare shoulder before rolling out of bed and walking into the bathroom to dispose of the condom. His heart was still pounding from the force of his release. He walked back into the bedroom and climbed back into the bed. After a moment's hesitation he pulled her into his arms.

She deserved that much. It didn't mean anything,

it couldn't. But it had been her first time, and she deserved to have nothing but good memories from it. She deserved more than he'd given her. More than he could ever give her.

He'd been counting on a second time, after he'd gotten the hot and fast out of the way. But he didn't want to cause her any pain.

In every possible way, he wanted to spare her pain. And he was worried that it was too late for that.

It was still dark when Lily opened her eyes. Gage's arm was snaked around her waist, holding her to him, her backside pressed against his hard erection.

She looked at the clock. Nearly five.

Panic fluttered in her stomach. She didn't want him to wake up and see her like she was. She needed her armor, something to help her be cool and calm when she had to face the man in whose arms she'd come apart. The man who knew she had been a twenty-seven-year-old virgin. The man who had held her while she'd cried in the aftermath of her release.

She slid out of the covers and she tiptoed out of the room and across the house, into her room, wishing, again, that there was a door so that she could close it behind her.

The first thing she did was check her email for new alerts and cursed creatively when she saw one pop up about Maddy.

She brainstormed ways to divert the new details Callahan and his wife were dishing while she showered, trying not to linger on the parts of her body that still felt sensitized from Gage's touch. She shivered as the hot water sluiced over her skin and tears pricked her eyes. Again. She shut the flow of water off and dried quickly, before applying her makeup, fixing her hair and picking out a freshly pressed skirt and button-up blouse.

She was sitting on the edge of the bed, fastening the dainty buckles on her blue kitten heels, when Gage's voice broke into her thoughts.

"You have the most interesting taste in shoes."

"I like shoes," she said, her heart fluttering wildly. She gritted her teeth and tried to calm her body's response to him before she looked up.

He was standing in the open doorway, leaning against the frame, wearing last night's jeans, riding low on his lean hips, and nothing else.

"Why aren't you in bed, Lily?" he asked, his voice so seductive it ought to be outlawed.

"I get up early," she said tightly, rising from her position on the bed. "And I'm not really a lounge-around-in-my-pajamas kind of person."

"I wouldn't guess you were. But I had hoped you were a walk-around-in-nothing-but-a-smile kind of person." His blue eyes were hot as he looked at her, his expression making it clear that, even though she'd gone to all the trouble to dress, he was envisioning her naked.

She sucked in a breath. "Nope, not that, either."

"Lily, come here."

She found herself walking toward him, even though she didn't remember telling her feet it was all right to move. He pulled her to him and kissed her, gently, seductively, sensually. She pressed her palms against his chest, intent on pushing away, but instead, her hands just lingered there, enjoying the feeling of all that hard, masculine flesh.

He pulled away slightly, resting his forehead against hers. "We aren't done," he said, his voice soft, but uncompromising.

Her whole body tingled, her nipples tightening, her core aching for his possession. They weren't done. There was no way she could leave it at one night, not when he still had the power to affect her like he did.

They had to let the fling run its course. That was what had to happen. They had a few days until they were meant to leave Thailand, and in that time they would be able to get it out of their systems. She was certain of it.

"I know we aren't," she whispered.

"When I wake up in the morning, I expect you to be in my bed. And I don't want you to be dressed." He moved against her, his arousal blatant, the intent in his eyes obvious. And she found herself responding to it. Very few men spoke to her that way. They found her intimidating. Gage didn't. And for some reason she found it incredibly sexy, hearing him say just what he wanted. "I want you naked. And I want you ready for me."

"I expect the same," she said, finding boldness much easier to come by when she had her appearance put together. It was easier to find her confidence when everything was in place. She felt more in her element, like this was a business negotiation and she had bargaining power.

"Those are terms I can readily agree to." He kissed her neck and she melted against him. "So, there is an advantage to you wearing your hair back. I can kiss you like this." He demonstrated again and she trembled beneath his erotic touch.

"I have some work to do this morning," she said, not sounding terribly convincing, even to herself.

"Do you?"

"Yes," she gasped as he nipped her lightly then soothed the sting away with his tongue. "A witness has spotted us venue-hunting for the wedding."

He stepped away. "Have they?"

She frowned. "I know. It's mildly horrible. But there are new details coming out about Maddy's supposed affair with William Callahan. If the media is intent on reporting that as fact with no more proof than they have, then I don't feel too guilty for misleading them."

"They're vultures. All they want is to feed off of the misfortune of others. To make a profit off of someone else's misery. I say lie away," Gage said, his expression fierce.

"Anyway, I just need to cultivate a convincing story and send it using one of my alternate email accounts."

"That's why I pay you so much."

"For my evil genius?"

He smiled, and her heart leapt. "Among other things." He cupped her cheek and her leaping, traitorous heart compounded its sins by pounding harder when he brushed his thumb lightly over her skin. "I'm going to go and check my email. I'll meet you afterward, for breakfast."

She could only nod as he turned and walked back out of the room. She sank onto the bed, hand on her chest, and tried to catch her breath. When he'd smiled like that…it had made her feel as if her heart was too big for her chest.

It's just the sex. Nothing more.

She walked over to the desk and sat at her laptop,

determined to push all thoughts of Gage from her mind and focus on her work. After all, the fling with Gage would only last a few more days. Her job was the constant. It was what mattered and she wasn't about to compromise that by trying to make more of their relationship than there could ever be. She didn't want it anyway.

The new physical connection they had was enough. She had no desire to get in any deeper. Part of her still wondered what she'd been thinking to give in to the attraction that burned between them. Part of her wished she'd just walked away from the edge of the cliff instead of jumping into the unknown.

He was right about one thing. She hadn't known. She'd thought sex would bring pleasure, but she hadn't realized the connection it could forge between two people, not really.

Of course, she hadn't been thinking when she'd agreed to the fling. She'd been following her most base desires instead of her intellect. Which had been her first mistake. But it was too late now. Now she *knew*. Now she felt like she had to let it reach a conclusion or it would always feel like it did now. Mysterious, almost too good to be real. Like she might cry just from thinking about the moment when Gage had joined his body to hers.

She finished dashing off the email and hit Send then leaned back in the chair, trying to breath deep enough to make the tightness in her chest go away.

She pushed away from the desk and stood. It was too late now. It was done. She'd made the decision, and she would accept everything that came with it. There was no point in regretting it. All she could do now was see it through. And when it was over she would be back to living like she always had, with the memory of how wonderful a few stolen moments in Gage Forrester's arms could be.

She managed to hold the tears back the second time they were together, until she escaped to her room on the excuse that she wanted a shower, and that she didn't want to share. Then she let it out. Tears tracked down her cheeks as she stood beneath the water.

She didn't know what it was that made her emotions, always so under control, release completely in the aftermath of a climax with Gage. She shut the water off and dried quickly, wrapping the towel tightly around herself before returning to the dark bedroom.

He'd honored her request for darkness this time, too, pulling down the shades likely because he knew just how inexperienced she was now. But he'd been merciless in his pursuit of giving her pleasure. He'd driven her higher, further, than she'd ever imagined possible.

And when she'd reached the peak, she'd screamed her pleasure. She cringed at the memory of how completely she'd lost her control. He'd always been able to do that to her. Even if it was just by getting her to talk about things she normally kept to herself.

She tiptoed back into the bedroom, hoping that Gage was asleep.

"You're beautiful," he said, his voice husky and enticing in the darkness, proving that her hopes for sneaking back in unnoticed were in vain.

A lot of men had told her she was beautiful, but never while she was naked. Not that he could see her all that well with the lamp switched off, the only light in the room filtering in from behind the edges of the shades. She was used to men drooling over her looks, but being told she was attractive had never affected her in the slightest.

It didn't matter what someone thought of her if she didn't have any interest in them. But hearing it from Gage made new heat bloom in her belly, made her ache to have him again, despite the strength of her earlier release. Physically, she was ready anyway. Emotionally, she didn't think she could go through it again.

She didn't respond, she only slid back into bed, her heart hammering already, just from being near him. She rolled over to her side, facing away from him, her arms crossed tightly over her breasts.

"You don't like to be told that you're beautiful?" She felt the mattress dip as Gage shifted and moved nearer to her, putting his arms around her and drawing her against him.

"Thank you," she said softly.

"You're so tense, Lily." He moved one hand to her shoulders and kneaded her tight muscles gently.

"I'm still not used to this."

Inwardly, Gage berated himself for putting both of them in this situation. He didn't know what compelled him to draw her closer, to want to comfort her when she was obviously in distress. It wasn't what he was looking for. But he couldn't resist the urge to hold her, either, even as slight panic gnawed at his stomach.

It was the responsibility that came with bedding a virgin. He'd never done it before that first night with Lily, and he wouldn't have done it if he would have had any idea that such a confident, sensual woman could have so little in the way of sexual experience.

Whether she believed him or not, she would remember him. Even he remembered his first lover and it had been nearly twenty-two years since the encounter. And it had only happened once. Like it or not, it was up to him to make sure she remembered her first times positively, since it would probably affect her future relationships.

He curled his arm more tightly around her as a fierce possessiveness, like nothing he'd ever felt before, coursed through him. He didn't want to think about Lily being with another man. Ever. She was his.

Mine.

He loosened his hold on her and rolled onto his back, gritting his teeth. She wasn't his. He didn't want her to be. She couldn't be.

He was having some sort of unforeseeable, uncontrollable response to being her first lover. Something he hadn't imagined he was capable of. He wasn't a traditional man. He was all for women being just as liberated as men when it came to sexual pursuits. Unless, of course, the woman was his sister. But he'd always sought out and preferred experienced women, so to have Lily's lack of experience mean anything to him didn't make any logical sense.

That he was bothered by her holding a part of herself back didn't make sense, either. But he was. He gave himself over to pleasure when they were in bed together, but he never engaged his emotions. For him, that wasn't a matter of holding back, that was simply how it was.

But after that first time, after that first, unexpected explosion of emotion, he sensed her fighting something, fighting him, each time they were together. He didn't want that. He wanted to draw the biggest response from her that he could, wanted to take her to new heights of pleasure every time. He wanted to steal all of her inhibitions, wanted her to make love to him in the bright light of day with her hair down and her body revealed to him.

He shouldn't want any of it, and none of it should matter. He had nothing to offer her. If he offered marriage what sort of prize would he be? A man who put his work before everything else. A man who would likely be just as good of a husband and father as his own father had been.

He drew her close to him again. Her virginity, her tears in the wake of a climax, none of it should matter. But it did.

CHAPTER NINE

THEY were leaving Thailand tonight, flying back to San Diego. Back to real life. Back to being boss and employee. Unless of course they were anywhere near where the media might be, then they were still an engaged couple. When they were really just a...not even a couple...just two people who had ended a recent, temporary, only physical fling.

Lily sighed and leaned back in her reclining chair, pretending to relax. That's what they were doing, relaxing, out on the island where they'd shared their first kiss. But she wasn't relaxed. She was aching inside and she wished, more than anything, that she wasn't. She wished she didn't feel anything. Maybe she should feel something, wistfulness maybe, a slight sadness that her incredible nights of pleasure were nearly over, but not this heaviness that had settled in her chest and made her entire being feel as if it was filled with lead.

Gage had been swimming, and she had been content to watch, studying his movements, his athleticism. Now, he was walking through the waves, making his way toward shore, his trunks resting low on his lean hips. And she couldn't help but admire him. Her lover. Her lover whose body she'd barely seen because she'd only ever consented to make love with him in the dark. She knew the feel of his body, though, knew the taste of it. Her heart tightened, and she ignored it.

He moved to her and sat beside her, his gaze roaming over her body, his eyes hungry. She wasn't as embarrassed this time, for him to see her in the bikini. She didn't even feel terribly self-conscious with her makeup washed off and her hair damp and curling thanks to her brief swim. She didn't need the shield as much as she had before.

"We're leaving tonight," he said, his voice husky.

"I know." She didn't look at him.

"Do you still want to end things when we leave Thailand?"

"It's for the best. We had a four-day fling, and it's over now. When we get back to San Diego it will be business as usual. And that's how it has to be, especially with everything going on concerning Maddy. I can't afford to be distracted, and neither can you."

"I do find you very distracting," he said. He leaned over her, brushed her hair from her face. "You're beautiful. I like the way you dress for work, but I like you like this, too. I especially like your freckles." He ran his finger lightly along the trail of dots that were sprinkled across the bridge of her nose.

She felt her cheeks heat. "I've never liked them."

"They're a part of your beauty." He brushed her cheek with the back of his hand and continued on, moving his knuckles lightly over her cleavage, barely hidden by the skimpy bathing suit. Her nipples puckered against the damp fabric, the slight chill created by the breeze not to blame for her response.

When he reached behind her and undid the knot on the halter top of the bikini she clamped her hands to her chest. "What are you doing?"

"Lily, I want to see you." His blue eyes were intense, compelling, his square jaw set.

She lowered her hands and let the fabric fall slightly, the lingering wetness keeping it from falling completely away.

"You don't need anything to be beautiful, sweetheart. All you need is to be you. You're the single most gorgeous woman I've ever seen."

His words were so sincere, and she felt them hit her straight in her heart, right at the source of the unbearable ache that had claimed her body for its own, reminding her that this was likely her last time with him.

The other times she'd been timid. She'd tried to hide behind darkness, behind her makeup, behind her business suits. But she wasn't going to hide anymore. She didn't need to. She was going to take this moment with Gage, this last moment, and she was going to simply feel all of the pleasure he could make her feel.

She pulled her top down the rest of the way and reached around behind herself, releasing the last knot holding the swimsuit on, the last thing keeping her from revealing her breasts.

Gage sucked in a sharp breath, his jaw clenched tight, his eyes hot on her, making her nipples ache for his touch. She hadn't realized how she would feel. She'd thought she would be relinquishing power by being naked, being so vulnerable in front of him. But instead, she just felt an incredible rush of power. The same way she had felt when she'd first realized how much he really wanted her.

He flexed his hands, tightened them into fists, and she knew that it was taking all of his restraint not to touch her, not to rush her. She met his gaze, arousal streaking through her, the abject desire so obvious in

Gage's eyes, in every tense line of his magnificent body, making her bold.

She moved so that she was on her knees and pressed her palms on his chest, still slick with water, hot from the sun, his heartbeat raging against her hand. "Take those off," she said, looking down at his shorts, at his erection, straining against the wet fabric.

He grinned at her, the wicked smile spreading slowly across his face as he moved his hands to the top of his shorts and pushed them down his spare hips, revealing his body fully to her for the first time.

She reached out and circled his shaft with her hand. "*You're* beautiful," she said.

"Now you," he said roughly.

She abandoned her hold on his body, gripped the sides of her bikini bottoms and dragged them down her legs, leaving them in the sand, any embarrassment she might have felt earlier completely absent now. She was lost, in the moment, in her feelings. In Gage.

She stood and wrapped her arms around his neck, kissing him, leading the kiss for the first time, adrenaline and desire pumping through her. "You have a condom, right?" she asked, panting heavily when she abandoned his mouth.

He chuckled and bent down, retrieving his shorts and producing a thin, plastic packet. "I wasn't a Boy Scout, but I take the motto very seriously."

"I'm glad."

He gave the condom packet to her and she tore it open without hesitation, hoping that the sense of confidence she was feeling would help where her inexperience might make things awkward. She was able to roll it onto his thick member without too much effort, the feeling of his hard flesh beneath her hand a thrill that she knew she could never tire of.

She kissed him, keeping her hand on his erection, squeezing him gently. He moaned into her mouth, his obvious appreciation more than enough to fuel the flame of her growing need.

"I want to be on top," she said, unsure if she'd really spoken the words out loud. But this was Gage. She had always spoken her mind to him. Why not now? This was her last chance to have him, and she wanted to have him on her terms. She wanted to have the control.

Gage was afraid he might be in danger of a heart attack, top physical condition or not. Lily, his shy lover, wasn't being shy now. He'd known she was beautiful, had admired what she'd allowed him to see of her body, and hadn't pressed for more out of deference to her in-experience. But now, she was gloriously naked in front of him, in the bright Thai sunlight, her breasts round and full, the tips peaked and aroused, rosy like her lips. A temptation he could not, and did not want to, resist.

He cupped them, teased them, teased himself until she whimpered with pleasure. "I want that, too, Lily," he said, his throat almost too tight for him to speak.

He gripped her around the waist and sat himself down on the sand, bringing her with him and settling her gently on top of him, her loose, wavy brown hair shielding them, creating a curtain around them.

He lifted his head and captured on of her perfect nipples between his lips and sucked gently. She gripped his shoulders and moved her hips, her feminine core sliding over his hard shaft. He cradled her hips and lifted her slightly, helping her find the right position. She sank down onto him gently, her head falling back and a moan of delight escaping her lips as he entered her fully.

It was a battle for him to stop himself from coming as soon as he was inside of her body. But the incredible feeling of being joined to her, combined with the full, unshielded vision of her gorgeous body, had him teetering on the brink.

His blood pounded through him, hard and hot, reckless. And when she began to move over him, setting a rhythm that was slow at first, then faster, more aggressive as she found exactly what pleased her, he could only hold tightly to her, using her hips to keep him anchored to the earth.

He felt her slick core tightening around him, felt the beginning of her orgasm. She bit her lip and tossed her head back again, fighting the release as she always did, before giving in and shuddering out her pleasure. As soon as she reached her peak, he gave himself permission to go over, giving in to his own release with a groan that he couldn't suppress.

She lowered her body onto him, her head resting on his shoulder, her breasts pressed tightly against his chest, her breathing harsh, shaky. He smoothed her hair back and wrapped his arms around her, enjoying the moment. He had never felt anything like that before, not in all of his years of experience.

He had always enjoyed sex, but it had been strictly physical. When he was with Lily it was beyond that. It went to a place that he had never imagined possible. A place he had never imagined could be remotely desirable.

He felt a strange tightening in his chest. She hadn't held back this time. She had been aggressive. She had given herself to him, not just her body, but something more. She had put serious insecurities to rest, and she had done it for him.

Part of him had wanted that, had resented that she'd withheld from him.

Now, with the unwanted tenderness swelling inside of him, all he could do was be thankful that this was their last time together. He couldn't afford for things to go further. For her to get in too deep with him. Because how could he ask all that he had from her, when he had nothing to offer in return?

It was impossible to sit next to Gage only hours after having him naked and beneath her and not have those images flash through her mind. He was back in his business suit, settled into his seat on the plane, his laptop open as he went over some of the specs for the hotel he was having built in England. Thoroughly in boss mode. And still she couldn't do anything but relive those last, powerful moments when she'd shattered over him, when only his tight grip on her hips had kept her from flying into a million pieces.

She hadn't cried that time. But everything in her had felt raw and exposed. She had felt so powerful at first, so amazed that she had been the one to make such a sexy man shake with need. But when her orgasm had crashed in on her she'd realized that if she had a hold on him, he had an equal hold on her. She'd thought she was in control, but it had been a false hope.

She'd also thought that a few days in Thailand would be enough to satisfy her curiosity, scratch her itch, or whatever she'd been imagining it to be. It was so much more complicated than that. She hated that it was, but the absolute truth was that she hadn't remained detached, and she didn't feel the same about him as she had when they'd first arrived in Thailand.

She didn't know how she felt, and, honestly, she didn't want to explore it. But she felt something.

"What are you working on?" she asked, feeling stupid and so much like the kind of silly female she'd always tried to avoid being. She knew what he was working on. It was a sad state of affairs when she was reduced to that kind of ridiculous behavior to make conversation.

"Just going over everything for the Hayden Hotel. Making sure everything I have in my database is the same as the report the contractor sent me."

"Oh," she said.

"It's getting late and we have to be in the office when we land in San Diego. You should try and get some sleep in one of the bedrooms."

By herself. Which she should be thrilled with since it was exactly in line with the deal they had made, and even if they were still involved in their purely physical relationship, she valued her space. But she wasn't thrilled. It made her chest ache, something she couldn't stop or understand.

"Okay. You should sleep, too." She didn't know why she'd said that. She sounded more like a nagging wife than an employee, or even a lover. *Attractive*.

He looked up from his computer and her breath caught. She blinked. He was handsome. He had been before they'd slept together, and he would undoubtedly continue to be handsome. He would probably only improve with age, since, unfairly, men seemed to do that. She couldn't afford to let him affect her every time he so much as glanced her direction.

"Later," he said.

There was no veiled promise in his words, no hint of anything more, like there would have been yesterday, or even earlier that day. He meant that later he would sleep, that was all.

And that was exactly what she would do, too.

She rose from her seat, brushed past him and went to the bedroom that was at the back of the plane. She selected the smaller of the two rooms, since it clearly wasn't the master bedroom, and that way she wouldn't run the risk of accidentally winding up in Gage's bed. Again. Not that any of the other times had been an accident.

Her heart rate kicked up at the thought, her breasts growing heavy, her body getting ready for another erotic encounter.

"Too bad," she said to the empty space.

She kicked off her shoes and lay down in the bed fully clothed, unwilling to go back out into the main part of the airplane and find her bags, which she'd forgotten to bring back with her.

She stretched out, telling herself that having the entire bed to herself was welcome, since she'd been forced to share her space for the better part of a week. But it didn't feel spacious, it felt cold and empty.

And she hated that, after only four days, it was stranger to be without him than it was to be with him.

CHAPTER TEN

"I THOUGHT you could use this," Lily said, setting the large coffee cup on Gage's desk. They were both suffering from jet lag, and even less sleep than usual. At least she was.

He, of course, appeared entirely unaffected as he looked up at her and offered a nod of thanks before accepting the coffee and taking a long drink. Only his closed eyes and slight sigh gave away just how much he needed it.

"What have you got for me this morning?" he asked, his eyes trained on his computer screen.

She took a breath. It was going to be fine. Easy. She was back in her element, not away at some sensual, tropical resort that was basically designed to make the patrons lose their minds and surrender to seduction.

"Nothing new regarding Maddy, but I wouldn't call off the engagement yet. Too obvious." She lowered her eyes and they settled on the ring, still in its place on her left hand. Her heart squeezed tight.

"Of course."

"Your wildlife sanctuary on Koh Samui is being hailed as a great act of conservationism. It's all over the news this morning."

"Good."

She gave him a hard glare. "You don't sound enthused."

"I told you, Lily—" he looked up at her "—my concern about my image begins and ends with the way it affects the bottom line. On a personal level, it isn't a priority." He looked back at his work.

"You're bullheaded, Gage Forrester," she mumbled, sitting in her chair and trying to ignore the rapid flutter of her heart that had been tormenting her since she'd woken up that morning.

"I see no real problem with that."

"What's wrong with people knowing you're a nice person?" she asked, exasperation edging its way into her voice.

"What's wrong with people I don't know and don't care about not knowing?"

She lowered her eyes and stared at the white lid on her coffee cup. "It doesn't make you like your parents just because the public knows about the good that you do in the world."

"We don't need to bring my parents into anything." She looked up into his ice-cold eyes. "It doesn't relate to the work we're doing here. You just stick to doing your job, Lily, and I'll do mine."

His parents and his past clearly wasn't open for discussion anymore. Not now that she was only an employee. When she'd been a potential lover he had shared with her, but now…now she wasn't fit to speak of it apparently. She sucked in a sharp breath. It didn't matter. He was right. It was personal, and this was business. What she'd learned about him during their brief relationship, if it could be called that, had nothing to do with what happened in their professional association.

She would just have to pretend that she didn't know

he'd sacrificed so much of his life to raise his sister, a sister he still felt responsible for. She'd have to pretend she didn't know exactly what he looked like under those perfectly tailored business suits.

Of course, it wasn't any kind of challenge for Gage. Temporary sexual relationships were par for the course for him. Which was one reason she'd decided to give a sexual relationship with him a try, so having an issue with it now was just contrary.

"All right, Gage, but it makes my job easier when you do as I advise you to do."

"I gave you my permission to make the announcement about the sanctuary," he said, his voice conveying just how unconcerned he was.

"Yes," she said tightly, "and it's helped. As I knew it would. Letting people run stories about you that are full of conjecture and false information isn't right."

"Of course, you have no trouble feeding the press false information."

She gave him a steely glare. "They had false information to begin with. And you didn't have a problem with it, either."

"To protect Madeline? Of course not. And we're going to continue on Saturday."

"Oh, really?" Her heart sped up.

"Yes. A very valuable client's daughter is getting married and holding the reception at the San Diego Forrester tomorrow. I've been asked to make an appearance, and of course that means my lovely fiancée should be on my arm."

She looked down at the ring that still glinted on her left hand, her entire body getting stiff with tension. It had been one thing to play happy couple with Gage before they'd been…intimate together. But it was quite another thing to try and pull off when that segment of their relationship was over.

She would have to touch him. Hold his hand. Maybe kiss him.

They hadn't held hands in Thailand. Not casually, not by themselves. It was an odd realization, and it was even stranger that she cared. It was simply a telling example of what their relationship had been. Purely sexual. Those little gestures that actual couples used to convey affection didn't apply to their four-day fling.

"Okay, that works for me." It did. It would. It had to. It was her job to protect Gage's image, and if she didn't go with him, questions might come up, which meant she had to go with him, and she had to turn in the performance of a lifetime.

It had meant buying a new dress—a short, black one with a low V-neckline that had a slight ruffle to help conceal some of the cleavage that the dress put on display—but when she walked into the San Diego Forrester on Gage's arm, her engagement ring sparkling in the overhead lighting, she felt like she belonged there. Like she belonged with Gage.

It was a dangerous feeling, but it was one she had to embrace, at least for the night. There was no other option. Tonight she was Gage Forrester's fiancée. She would try not to focus on the fact that she was really Gage Forrester's discarded leftovers.

Who asked to be discarded.

She took a deep breath and tried to rid herself of the tightness in her chest.

The hotel was decorated beautifully, every table covered with a crimson tablecloth, white orchids in white vases acting as centerpieces. And the tablecloths matched her shoes, which was a very nice and convenient surprise.

Maybe if she focused on that she would survive the evening with some semblance of sanity intact.

Gage put his arm around her waist the moment they fully entered the reception area and she had to fight the urge to melt against him. It was so strange, how natural it was to want that. How easy it was to want to lean on him.

She managed to stop herself. She wasn't about to cling to him, even if his touch did feel better than she remembered. And he smelled amazing. She'd always noticed that about him, from the very first time they'd met. But it was different now, more intimate. Now she picked up on the subtle scent of his skin…clean, but beneath the scent of soap and aftershave, the slight musk of his skin. She could pick it out so easily now, now that she'd been so close to him, now that she knew just how his skin tasted.

The thought made her want to moan out loud, but she managed to hold it back.

Gage sought out the father of the bride and he introduced Lily as his fiancée, then talked to the man for a while about the reception, and offered a free round of drinks. After that, he was fielding requests to hold events at the hotel from every third guest they encountered.

"That was clever," Lily said as they took their seat at their own private table.

"My hotels are popular for a reason."

"You know how to give good service," she said lightly, not realizing the undercurrent in her words until it was too late. And then their eyes met and her stomach tightened.

She licked her lips, but as soon as she slicked her tongue across them they were dry again. She wondered if he could see the signs of her arousal. He knew her so well in that way. She could see his. His eyes darkened, a muscle in his jaw jumped, his hand tightening around his wineglass. He wanted her, too, even though their fling was over.

He'd been cool on the plane ride back to the U.S. and in the office over the past week, but it had been a show. She'd assumed he was done with her, that he'd consigned their affair to a pleasant memory and hadn't thought of her that way, hadn't wanted her, since the moment they'd left Thailand.

"I meant, your customer service is outstanding," she said tightly, trying to ignore the pounding of her pulse and the rush of blood that was making her body feel ultrasensitive.

"Of course," he said, his voice rough, his arousal obvious to her.

"This is really beautiful," she said, trying to recover from her foot-in-mouth moment.

"Yes, it is." His eyes were fixed on her, his gaze lingering on the swell of her breasts. She'd chosen the dress partly for that reason, she was ashamed to admit. She'd told him once that she didn't pick her clothes based on someone else's desires, but she had today. She knew that he liked her figure, and she'd set out to elicit a response from him.

But it was so frustrating, seeing him the office, burning for him, while he seemed to feel nothing but professional courtesy. She was frustrated with him, and she was frustrated with herself. She didn't know what she wanted, didn't know what response the wanted him to give her. She just knew she was unhappy, that at night her bed felt cold and empty. That she no longer found solace in her beachfront apartment and her solitude.

"Gage…"

He reached across the table and captured her hand in his, stroking it lightly with his fingers. She closed her eyes and let out a slow breath, electricity sparking in her body, her heart beating double time, everything in her shaking with desire.

"I've been thinking a lot about you, Lily. About our time in Thailand."

"Don't," she said sharply, pulling her hand back and putting it in her lap.

"You tried to deny the attraction between us before, Lily, and it couldn't be done."

She swallowed hard. "We can ignore it. I can ignore it."

He looked at her, those blue eyes more temptation than she could handle. "But do you want to ignore it?"

"No," she whispered.

"Then what do you want?"

He was going to make her say it. For the first time in her life she wished someone would make things easy for her. That he would just sweep her into his arms and carry her up to one of the suites. But he was making her choose. He was leaving the consequences up to her, which meant that later, she wouldn't be able to blame him if things exploded on them.

"I want you," she said, her voice low, "but I don't want to want you."

"That does amazing things for my ego, sweetheart," he said, offering her a slight smile.

Her heart tripped and a short laugh escaped her lips. "You know I'm not into ego stroking, Gage."

"That's a shame." Their eyes caught and held, tension and electricity arcing between them.

"One more night." Her words were rushed, the blood roaring in her ears.

"One more night," he said, standing from the table, taking her hand and drawing her up with him.

"Isn't it rude to leave this early?" She cast a backward glance at the full reception, at the cake that had yet to be cut.

"It's not as rude as my stripping your dress off of you and having my way with you in front of all those nice people would be."

They headed down one of the long hallways to a row of elevators.

"You wouldn't do that," she said, going for censorious, but only managing breathless.

"I never thought I would, Lily, but you make me feel things…" He trailed off and stopped walking, turning her so that her back was to the wall. He stepped in, put his hands on her waist and leaned in, taking her mouth, devouring her as though he was starving. "You make me do things," he said. "I don't know myself sometimes when I'm with you."

"Same here," she said weakly, the wall and Gage's hands the only thing keeping her from sliding to the carpeted floor.

"My apartment is here," he said, "at the hotel."

"Really?"

"It made things easier to manage, especially in the beginning. I've never left." He punched the "up arrow" button on the wall and the elevator doors slid open. "Spend the night with me."

"Yes."

He stepped into the elevator and pulled her in with

him, holding her tightly against his body, kissing her neck softly.

"Gage," she whispered, wrapping her arms around him and taking his lips with hers. She'd missed him, much more than she'd realized, much more than she wanted to face.

He backed her up against the wall, the kiss growing urgent, hungry. She gripped the knot of his tie and jerked it hard to the side, loosening it so that she could reach the top button of his dress shirt and unfasten it with her shaking fingers.

She slid her hand inside his shirt, curling her fingers when she came into contact with his hot, hard flesh. He growled and gripped her hips, drawing her tightly against him. There was no restraint in him this time. Always before, he'd held back, but now he was unleashed and she was experiencing the full force of his desire. She gripped the edges of his shirt and tugged, sending buttons scattering across the elevator floor.

She slid her hands down his stomach, over his perfect ab muscles. He was so beautiful to her. Her heart thundered and she felt an intense well of emotion stir in her stomach, mingling with the intense desire to have him inside of her, to be joined to him again.

Gage gripped the sides of her dress and bunched it up in his hands, and Lily felt the hem rise higher. "Are you trying to kill me, Lily?" he groaned when his hands made contact with the bare space of skin between her black thigh-high stockings and her thong panties.

"That wasn't my goal. If you're dead you'll be of no use to me."

He laughed wickedly and kissed the curve of her neck, his fingers edging beneath the thin fabric of her underwear. She gasped when he moved his fingers over her clitoris.

"Is that good?" he asked, his lips brushing against her sensitized skin.

She could only nod as he continued to work magic on her with his hands. He slid one finger inside of her and felt a surge of pleasure, a tightening in her pelvis that she knew meant her climax was about to crash in on her.

"Come for me," he whispered, adding a second finger, and she was powerless to do anything but obey.

She gripped his shoulders, her hands still beneath his destroyed shirt, her nails grazing his sweat-slicked back.

When she finally came back to reality she realized they were still in the elevator.

"I stopped it," he said, gesturing to the control panel.

She adjusted her dress and patted her hair with a shaking hand. "Good." She had forgotten. She'd forgotten everything but how much she wanted him. She'd forgotten self-preservation, common decency, everything.

And she couldn't regret it. Not yet. Because even though her body was still tingling with the aftereffects of her orgasm, she wanted more. She wanted him. All of him.

He pushed the button for the top floor and the elevator began to move again. When they reached the top floor he keyed in a code and the doors slid open, revealing an extremely masculine, modern apartment space.

She stepped out of the lift on wobbly legs. She felt a slight smile tug at the corners of her mouth. The whole place was very Gage. Furniture with clean lines, neutrals accentuated by pops of color that reminded her of the beach. It was beautiful and opulent, and surprisingly functional.

It felt more intimate now, being in his home. It was one thing to have an affair at a vacation spot, but another to actually come into where he lived. To sleep in his bed.

Panic nibbled at her, her stomach about to explode in a flurry of nerves. But then Gage put his arm around her and dipped his head to give her a light kiss on the lips, and she couldn't worry anymore. Relationships, feelings, commitment, all of it scared her, made her want to run. But Gage didn't. Somehow, no matter what the feelings between them were, she couldn't be afraid of him.

"Would you like something to drink?"

She laughed. "Not yet. We have unfinished business." She looked at him, at his gaping shirt that was still tucked into his slacks. "I like the look," she said.

"I was attacked by a shameless hussy in an elevator," he said, taking her hand and leading her down the hallway.

He had pictures on his wall. School pictures of Maddy. Her high school and graduation pictures. It hit her again what a wonderful man he was, the things that he chose to hide. Part of her wanted to find out everything, but so much of her wanted to ignore everything she already knew, and didn't want to find out any more. This was about sexual satisfaction, a slight extension on their fling's deadline. This wasn't about finding out what an incredible person he was.

His bedroom was a definite man cave. A large bed, wall-mounted TV and very little else. Not the den of seduction she'd always imagined. She'd sort of thought he might be the type to have a Jacuzzi tub and a stripper pole in the middle of his bedroom. She was relieved to see she'd been wrong. Not that it should matter.

He shrugged his shirt off and tossed it onto the floor, his slacks and underwear following. She reached around to grab the zipper tab on her dress.

"Wait a second," he said, coming toward her. "Let me."

He turned her around gently so that she was facing away from him, his hands possessive on her hips. She leaned back against him, reveling in his heat, his strength. In him.

He slid his hands up beneath her dress and gripped her panties, dragging them down her legs. She stepped out of them and kicked them aside, trying to make sure they didn't get caught on her heels.

He moved his hands to her waist, slid them over her hips, back up to her breasts, not really touching, not the way she wanted. It was as though he was tracing her curves, memorizing her shape.

Then he slowly pulled the zipper down and she let her dress fall to the floor. A masculine groan of appreciation rumbled in his chest. "You're gorgeous," he groaned. "The most beautiful woman I've ever seen. I'll never get enough of looking at you."

Her heart thundered, her body quivering with desire. "Gage," she choked out.

"Get on the bed," he said, his voice rough, commanding, thrilling.

She complied, trying to turn and face him.

"No," he said, moving behind her and taking one of the pillows from the head of the bed, then another, stacking them and moving her over them so that her upper body had some support.

Her blood rushed through her veins, hotter, faster. She knew what he was going to do, and it thrilled her, excited her and frightened her, all at the same time.

"Do you trust me, sweetheart?"

She could only nod, the lump in her throat too much for her to speak past. But she did trust him. In this moment she did. She was giving him more than she'd ever given to anyone else, and as much as it scared her, it also felt as necessary as breathing.

She heard him tearing a condom packet, protecting them both, as he always did. She was grateful for that. She knew a lot of men didn't care enough to do that, but Gage never acted as though it was a sacrifice, as though it should be up to her.

She felt the blunt head of his erection probing her slick entrance.

"Are you ready for me?" he asked.

"Yes," she managed to choke out.

He thrust inside of her, deep, deeper than she'd ever felt him before. She curled her fingers around the bedspread, trying to hold back the hoarse cry of pleasure that was climbing her throat.

He held her hips tightly, his movements strong and sure, nothing tentative about his claiming of her body. Because that was what it felt like. It was more elemental than their other times together, and in a lot of ways, she had less control. She was at his mercy, and yet she couldn't be afraid of him, and he wasn't harming her, he was only giving to her. Giving her pleasure while he took his own. While they shared in it.

He reached around and stroked the source of her desire. Already she could feel another orgasm building, this one stronger, more intense. She whimpered, and clenched the comforter tighter, the tension too much for her to bear because she knew when it broke she would shatter with it.

She felt his muscles start to shake, felt his fingers dig into her hips. He was close, too.

"Lily," he said, as he went over the edge.

His fingers worked her faster and she followed him, her body tightening around him as he pulsed inside of her. Their orgasm went on and on, blended together until she was sure they were feeling the same thing. Until it almost felt as though they were one body.

And when it was over, he turned her and took her in his arms so that she was facing him, so that he could brush her hair out of her face, his other hand continually sliding over her curves.

"Did you like that?" he asked. There was no arrogance in his voice. He didn't behave as though he already knew the answer, he wanted to know. And that made her heart squeeze tightly in her chest. Gage wasn't the kind of man who questioned himself, and that he would do it for her...it was impossible to feel nothing.

"Very much. It was incredible."

He circled her waist with his arms, bringing her closer, and she curved her leg over his thigh. They just lay there for a moment, catching their breath, letting their heart rates return to normal.

"This isn't the way I pictured your bedroom," she said finally.

"Really? What did you picture?"

"Stripper pole."

He laughed and kissed her hair. "Sorry to disappoint. For you, I would have one installed, trust me. The possibilities are fascinating."

She smiled against his shoulder. Surprisingly, the idea of putting herself on display for him like that didn't horrify her in the least. How could it when they'd shared so much?

"I don't bring women here," he said.

"Could have fooled me."

"You're actually the first woman I've had here since Maddy came to live with me. I got used to conducting my affairs away from my home. I don't even have them in my own hotels."

"Why is that?"

His body tensed slightly. "Probably for the same reason we both live alone."

"Then why...why did you bring me here?"

He shrugged. "You're different. I know you. I was feeling very impatient."

Her stomach tightened. His words thrilled her and scared her. She was different. He knew her. He had brought her back to his apartment, a place he didn't bring other women.

She wasn't supposed to be different. She was supposed to be another in a long string of purely physical affairs, a woman he wouldn't want anything from. And she was supposed to feel the same way about him. He wasn't supposed to matter.

Of course she liked him, but there couldn't be anything beyond that.

She should get up. Get dressed and go home. He would probably expect it. He should expect it. It was different when they were both staying in Thailand. But here in San Diego they both had their own houses, their own space.

But he was still cradling her against his chest, and for some reason, even though he was the source of her fear, he was also a source of comfort. She wrapped her arms around him and rested her head on his chest. Nothing had changed. It was just a part of their fling. It couldn't be anything more.

CHAPTER ELEVEN

"I THOUGHT you could use some." Gage held a mug of coffee out to Lily and she sat up straighter in the bed, letting the covers fall around her waist.

"Thank you," she said, taking it and inhaling the heavenly scent. She was such an addict, but at least he understood. Understood and shared in it.

It was an interesting reversal of their morning routine. And an interesting setting for it. She'd always thought there was an undercurrent of domesticity in their office routine, but this took it to a whole new level.

He sat on the edge of the bed, his own mug in hand, dressed only in a pair of jeans, his chest still bare. There were certain aspects of this that were a definite improvement to their office mornings.

"What are your plans for the day?" she asked, a little embarrassed once the question had escaped. Was it really any of her business what he was doing? It wasn't a workday and they didn't have a real relationship.

"Nothing. A total rarity. Usually I try to visit Maddy on Sunday, but she's still in Switzerland, and having a lot of fun. She says she's been totally untouched by the scandal there."

"That's great, Gage." She could see the relief on his

face and it made her feel the same feeling, swelling inside of her. She knew how much he loved Maddy, knew even more now. She felt as though she could feel his emotions sometimes, as though her own matched his.

Gage was enjoying Lily's newfound boldness in bed. Even now she was sitting up with her breasts bare, acting as though she hardly noticed. He noticed. She was truly the most beautiful woman he'd ever seen naked. And he'd seen his share.

Usually, after a few encounters, the mystery had worn off and he wasn't as captivated by his lover's beauty. Or, as was the case when plastic surgery was involved, sometimes a woman actually looked better in her clothes than out of them.

But not Lily. She fascinated him. Clothed or naked, dressed up, or in a bikini.

He kept waiting to regret bringing her back to his apartment, letting her into his personal space. But it hadn't hit him yet. It felt better, having her here than it would have felt taking her to an anonymous hotel and having sex with her on a bed that was there almost solely for that purpose.

It had never bothered him before. That was how he'd always conducted his affairs. If it weren't for those years raising his sister, his room may very well have ended up with a stripper pole in it. But he *had* raised his sister, and that had changed things. It had likely changed some things for the better.

He didn't know what was happening with Lily. Didn't want to know why it felt right to have her in his home, when he had never wanted to bring another woman here before. Didn't want to know what it meant that he couldn't imagine ever tiring of her.

Last night had been the hottest night of his life, hands down. The only other experiences that came close were the other times he'd been with Lily. She wiped memories of other women from his mind. He couldn't even remember what appeal those other women had ever held. They were too blonde, too tanned, too thin, too surgically enhanced. There was nothing genuine about them.

They weren't like Lily. Lily, who was soft and beautiful, who didn't cling to him. Lily, who he gladly held all night long, when he'd never wanted to do that with any other woman.

"I need to go home," she said suddenly.

His first thought was that he didn't want her to leave. And he'd definitely never felt that way about a woman before. He hated to admit that that first reaction, the desire to hold her to him, keep her with him, scared him.

There was no point in caring. No point in wanting.

"Why?"

"I don't have any clothes. I only have that dress." She gestured to the black fabric pooled at the foot of his bed. "And when I leave, everyone's going to know what was going on. No one wears a dress like that on Sunday morning."

"My simple solution is that you could forgo clothes altogether."

"No."

"I'll drive you back to your place. Is there anything else you need?" he asked.

"I usually work out today."

He wasn't surprised to know that she worked on her body. She took a lot of care with her appearance, not to the point of obsession, but just enough that she projected a very polished image. That was one thing that made ruffling her so much fun.

And if he could just focus on the fun and ignore all of the other things, their affair could continue for as long as they both wanted.

"I'll go with you. I work out on Sundays, too."

She nodded slowly, but he could tell she wasn't thrilled with the idea. She was extremely cagey and very closed off with her emotions, something he normally wouldn't notice or care about, but for some reason, with her, he cared.

When they were in bed together, or on the beach, her walls started to come down, and he reveled in those moments. He shouldn't. There was nowhere for their relationship to go. Even if he wanted love and marriage, she was the wrong woman. What could they bring to a marriage? A mutual obsession with their own businesses, their own lives? And if he didn't have his business, what other attraction could he possibly offer?

In business, they were well-suited, in bed, they were incredible. But that was all it would ever be. That was all it could ever be.

"Remind me never to work out with you again," Lily said, rubbing her shoulders as she settled into Gage's low-slung sports car.

"Too much for you?"

She groaned and leaned her head back against the seat. "Normally, I don't like to admit defeat, but in this case, I'll concede."

"Are you hungry?" Gage asked, maneuvering the car into traffic.

"Very."

"Do you want to go out?"

She grimaced. After a workout that intense, she wasn't fit to be out in public. "I can cook for you. My condo is close."

Gage hesitated for a moment before changing lanes and heading in the direction of her home. She didn't know what she was doing, why she was inviting him to come home with her. Because she was certain that he would end up staying. That they would end up in bed together, and she was sure that was the wrong thing to do. She should have told him to drop her off at home, should have tried to start putting distance between them.

But she hadn't. And even now that she recognized what she should do, she wasn't going to do it. She wanted to be with him. Maybe she should stop analyzing everything and just be with him.

"It's a two-car garage," she said when he pulled into the lot of her condo. "Just stop here for a second."

She got out of the car and keyed in the code for the garage and the door opened. She got back into the car while Gage drove it inside, parking next to her little commuter vehicle. For a moment, it seemed shockingly comfortable, to have his car parked next to hers, almost like they shared the space.

She shook her head and got back out of the car and moved to unlock her side entrance. Gage followed her in. She had always been proud of her house, and had hosted a few dinner parties for her friends when she'd had the time, not since she'd started working for Gage. It wasn't as luxurious as his house, but it was hers.

"You have a view of the ocean from here?" he asked.

"From the bedroom."

"I'll have to take a look," he said, giving her a wicked grin.

"Later," she said, "but now I'm hungry."

"Later," he said, hooking his arm around her waist and bringing her in for a kiss. He hadn't kissed her at all today. They'd spent the day together but he hadn't touched her, hadn't acted like there was anything between them. She was surprised by how much she'd missed it.

"Definitely." She moved away from him and went into the kitchen and started rifling through the produce drawers in her fridge. "Stir-fry?" she asked.

"I didn't imagine that you would cook."

"I have to eat."

"My mother didn't cook."

Lily laughed, but there was no humor in it. "Neither did mine." She put a head of cabbage on her cutting board and began to slice it. "I learned when I moved out here. Otherwise I existed on frozen pizza and whatever my friends' parents fed me when they felt sorry for me."

"Do you have any family here?"

"No. I left home at seventeen. My main requirement was that none of my family be where I went," she said, hearing the bitterness edge into her voice.

"And you wanted to be near the ocean," he said.

"Yes. I did."

"Did the men your mother dated hurt you? Is that why you avoided relationships?"

She took a breath and tossed the sliced cabbage into the wok on the stove. "They didn't hurt me in the way that you mean. But my mother was so dependent on them, and most of them were terrible. She let them control everything she did, and by extension, everything

I did. We always lived in these tiny little houses with no privacy. I could always hear them fighting, or making up. I'm not sure which was worse."

She put the rest of the vegetables and some pre-cooked chicken into the wok and pushed them around vigorously with a spatula for a few minutes before turning the burner off.

"Not all relationships are like that," he said.

"Not all of them are like your parents', either."

He didn't say anything to that. Conversation turned back to business, and she was thankful for that.

She served their dinner in the dining room and Gage sat in the chair next to her, instead of sitting across from her, his hand on her thigh, stroking her absently. It was very domestic, the two of them eating a dinner she'd cooked. It certainly didn't fit in to the parameters of an affair.

Neither did sharing the gory details about a dysfunctional childhood. But Gage had always made her want to open up. It had always been easy for her to say too much to him.

They ended up watching a movie in the living room before heading to her bedroom and making love. It was amazing, like it always was, and, like always, she felt a little piece of the wall around her heart crumble when she came apart in his arms.

And when he gathered her against him she felt tears trailing down her cheeks again, all of the emotion rising up inside of her again, needing a way to escape.

She didn't know what it was that made her feel this way. Not for sure. She had a suspicion, but she hoped, more than anything, that she was wrong.

* * *

They drove to the office together the next day, despite her protests. She also conceded to packing an overnight back, just in case. She shouldn't have. She shouldn't have left it open. She should be ending it. They'd had an agreement and they weren't sticking to it.

The relationship, because it was growing into that, was now beyond her control. She wanted to be with Gage almost more than she wanted her next breath, but she didn't want to want it. She didn't want to want him.

She was sitting in her spot in his office, notebook in hand as he briefed her on a new resort property in Goa, India.

"Any concerns regarding the location?" she asked.

"Not that I can foresee. It's an older resort, and basically we'll be renovating it and bringing some more tourism into the area."

"Excellent. I love it when you make my job easy." She looked up at him and her heart fluttered in her chest.

There was no compartmentalizing. She had thought that Gage, her lover, could be someone different in her mind than Gage, her boss. After all, she'd always been able to set everything aside and focus on her work. But it wasn't possible. Whenever she looked at him she was flooded by memories of them making love, of him looking at her, his expression tender.

"And I don't do it very often," he said.

"You're getting better."

"Don't let that get out."

She smiled. "I won't."

Gage stood from his desk and walked around to where she was sitting, coming to stand behind her before leaning down and kissing her lightly on the neck. "You're a terrible workplace distraction."

She closed her eyes. She knew he was making a joke. But it was true for her. He was distracting. She couldn't think about her job when she was with him. She could only think about him.

"I want to take you out tonight," he whispered, his hands moving over her shoulders, sparking a fire in her belly.

"You took me out a few days ago. To the wedding reception."

"No, I want to take you out on a date. Not to a work event designed for networking."

"Why? So we can have our picture taken together?"

"It wouldn't hurt."

It was important, of course. Gage was always seen in public with his woman *du jour,* and it wouldn't do for his fiancée to be the exception.

"All right. What do you want to do? And do I need a new dress?" she asked.

"It's a surprise, and I've taken care of everything for you. You'll come home with me after work, just like we planned."

She moved away from his touch and stood. "Then I'd better get to work."

He cupped her chin and kissed her lightly on the lips. "See you later."

She smiled, and she was afraid it was a little bit of a punch-drunk smile. "See you later."

She didn't need to buy a new dress, because there was already one waiting at Gage's home for her. It was on his bed, zipped up into a garment bag.

"Did you pick this out or did David?" she asked, turning to face Gage, who was standing in the doorway.

"David has terrible fashion sense. I chose it at lunch, but I sent a picture of it to Maddy to make sure it was right."

It felt a little strange letting him pick out her clothes. She'd never liked it when any of her friends chose an outfit around a boyfriend, or let him dictate their wardrobe. Of course, she was already starting to think of Gage when she shopped. And he wasn't even her boyfriend, not really. *Boyfriend* was too insipid of a word for a man like Gage. *Lover* was more accurate, and more fitting. More arousing.

"I want to see how it looks on you." He stood there, eyes fixed on her.

"Not with you standing there."

"I've seen you naked before," he said dryly. "I hope that's not a shocking revelation for you."

"It's different than getting changed in front of someone."

"It is?"

She nodded. "Yes, it is. So…" She gestured for him to go.

"I'll go, only because I was taught it was polite not to impose on a lady, but, and this is a promise, I will be stripping that dress from your delectable body later, which renders this show of modesty entirely worthless."

"Then it's worthless." She turned away from him, then said, "I hope you're a man who keeps his promises."

"Always." The door clicked shut behind her and she turned again. Gage was gone, giving her the privacy she'd asked for.

She bent down and unzipped the bag. And laughed. It was bright red, made in a heavy satin fabric, the exact opposite of the type of thing she normally wore. No black, no navy, nothing flowing. Of course. She would have been annoyed, but she appreciated his humor too much.

And the dress was gorgeous, which further absolved him. The sweetheart neckline was sexy, but not overt, which earned him major points since he could have gone plunging. The hem fell just above her knee and there was exquisite pleating at the waist that was extremely flattering to her figure.

There were shoes, too. Black, of course, to defy her usual affinity for colorful shoes. And she found she liked the shoes as well as the dress.

She emerged from the bedroom dressed, her hair down, another style choice she didn't usually make. "Will this do?" she asked.

Gage stood from where he was sitting on the couch, his expression intense, his eyes roaming over her, the hunger in them compelling, undisguised.

"You're gorgeous," he said. "Have I mentioned that?"

Yes, he had, and every time it felt more and more real. "Once or twice."

"I thought you might appreciate the color choice."

"It was clear you had my tastes in mind when you picked it. And then decided to go with the opposite. But I do like it."

"I'm glad, because I'm a big fan."

He stood and walked over to her, looping one arm around her waist and then moving his other hand to her loose hair, sifting it through his fingers. "You have beautiful hair. I'm captivated by it."

She sucked in a breath. "You're an easy man to captivate."

"No," he said, his face serious, "I'm not." He lowered his head and kissed her lightly, the gesture somehow more romantic than if he'd ravished her mouth.

"I'm almost ready," she said, knowing she sounded as breathless as she felt. "Makeup."

He followed her into the bathroom and grabbed his razor from the medicine cabinet while she rummaged through the bag she'd brought with her and found a shade of red lipstick that would work well with the dress.

He shaved away his five-o'clock shadow while she put the finishing touches on her look, and the whole time her hands were shaking. It was the sort of thing a married couple would do. At least, the sort of thing she imagined a normal married couple might do.

"I'm ready," she said. Anything to get away from the house, from this domestic scene that was making her whole body ache with longing she didn't want to feel.

All eyes were on them as they made their way to a trendy San Diego nightspot. It was because of Gage, she was certain. He drew the attention of men and women. It was more than just his incredible looks, though they were certainly a factor, it was the aura of power that he projected.

He went straight past the maître d' and led her to a table in the back. "My table," he said, as he pulled her chair out for her. It was secluded, set back into an alcove that had a curtain just barely drawn back so that the main portion of the dining room was mostly hidden from view.

"You come here often?" she asked facetiously.

"It's one of my favorite places."

She wasn't sure how she felt about coming to a place he went to with other women. She couldn't feel anything about it. It couldn't matter. They were here to get attention from the press and the fact that it was one of his usual places made it a good choice to accomplish that. Everything else was moot.

But it didn't feel like it. It felt vital somehow.

"Our food will be here shortly," he said.

"You ordered ahead? And without asking what I wanted?"

"No, I always get whatever fresh item they're featuring on the menu and they know that."

The little flutter of panic that had been ready to take flight in her stomach calmed slightly. It was only food, but there was the dress, too, and the shoes. It was the kind of thing she'd always worried about when it came to men and relationships.

He reached across the table and squeezed her hand, just as the waiter was coming with their dinner. She had to wonder if he had done it because he wanted to, or if it was part of the show. She couldn't worry about it though, not when he was looking at her like she was the only woman he wanted. Like she was the only woman he'd ever wanted.

He was the only man she would want. She couldn't imagine being with anyone else. Couldn't imagine wanting to be. She'd never met a man to equal him before, and she doubted she ever would. She ignored the trickle of fear she felt as she acknowledged that. Until that moment she'd been pretending that she would simply find someone else when she was ready. When she had physical needs again.

It was a reasonable thought. If she and Gage were

only fulfilling a physical need for each other, then wouldn't anyone do?

No.

"It's hard to enjoy dinner when all I want is to take you back home make love with you."

Lily blushed, something Gage found infinitely attractive. That she was capable of the act at all was a novelty, but that wasn't what it was. It was more than that. With Lily it was always more. He'd attributed it to her being a virgin, but it wasn't so simple.

Tonight, when she'd walked out of the bedroom in that red dress, he'd known for sure there was more. He wasn't entirely certain what he was going to do about it, a first for him, but he knew that she wasn't simply a temporary diversion. Knew that it wasn't about distracting the press anymore, or even a simple fling. They had passed that point a long time ago.

She looked at him, her expression wicked. "I'm having similar fantasies involving your shirt."

"You've already ruined one of my favorite shirts."

"It's for the greater good," she said, a smile curving those lush red lips.

He loved talking with Lily, loved the way her mind worked, her wit, her sense of humor. Her company. There had never been anyone in his life who added so much. She understood his business, she was wonderful to talk to, and in bed…he had never experienced anything like what they shared when they were together.

Usually by now, he would be bored with a lover. But he couldn't imagine Lily boring him in any way. And he didn't know what that meant, what purpose it could possibly serve. He didn't know how to give love, didn't know how to receive it. There was Maddy, but she loved him because she'd always needed him. He had no experience with the emotion otherwise. He seriously doubted he was capable of giving it or getting it.

But for now, it didn't matter. He wouldn't let it. Tonight he would lose himself in her body again. Tonight he would be inside of her, and when that happened, nothing else seemed to matter quite so much.

They both ate quickly, all thoughts of a photo-op for the press forgotten, and as soon as he paid the check they made a mad rush for his car.

He took her hand and she laughed, walking quickly in her heels. He spun her to him and kissed her, his stomach tightening when she pulled away and he got a good look at her gorgeous face, at her beautiful smile.

"We should hurry," he said, his constricted throat making speech a near impossibility.

"I agree."

CHAPTER TWELVE

BEING with Gage, making love with Gage, was always amazing. But it had never been like this. His hands moved over her curves, his touch reverent, his lips soft but urgent on her skin. And when he claimed her, surged into her body, she truly felt as though she didn't know where she began and he ended.

She dug her nails into his shoulders, locked him more tightly against her by wrapping her legs around his hips and she arched into him and gave in to the pleasure that was coursing through her body. But it was more than that. More than just a physical reaction brought on by sexual arousal and release.

His body went taut above hers, the tendons in his neck standing out, a hoarse grunt signaling his orgasm. She held him to her, felt his heart beating hard against her chest. It was so much more than sex. So much more than a fling.

And she didn't think she could face it.

Before she and Gage had started sleeping together, they'd been colleagues, they'd almost been friends and then they'd moved into being lovers. But now it had moved beyond that. There was so much more. It made her heart feel like it was too big for her chest, made her entire body ache. And it also made her feel more alive than she'd ever been. And it terrified her.

She shifted beneath him and he rolled off of her, settling beside her. She squeezed her eyes tightly, hoping that she wasn't about to embarrass herself by crying postclimax again. Only this time it wouldn't simply be due to the release. It was all about the feelings that were exploding inside of her.

Gage gathered her close and she went willingly into his arms. Even though it seemed necessary to her control that she have some distance, she just couldn't bring herself to leave. She wanted to be with him.

He laced his fingers through her and kissed her shoulder, the gesture one of tenderness, caring. A gesture that made it hard for her to breathe.

"Thank you for what you've done for Maddy," he said, his voice rough, his breathing harsh.

She felt a twinge in her chest. She didn't want what had just happened between them, what had been happening between them for the past couple of weeks, to be her thank-you for helping out his sister.

"Of course," she said, trying to keep her voice steady.

"She's had to deal with enough without adding this…I can never forgive my parents for what they've done to her." He tightened his hold on her. "The worst part is, I would be an even worse father than my own was."

She turned to face him. "Why do you think that?"

"My work is my mistress. And just like a real mistress, it tends to get in the way of your real family."

"But you raised Madeline."

He nodded. "I did. And I wouldn't trade it. She's

wonderful. But I put a lot on hold for her and if I were going to have children I would have to do it again."

She nodded. "That's true."

"You don't want kids, do you?"

She bit her lip, the flow of emotion that was pumping through her a mystery. "No. I have the same problem with my job that you have."

She'd never planned on having children, never wanted to get married, but suddenly, the idea seemed sad to her. Listening to Gage outline just why it was impractical for either of them to ever have a family made everything seem so final. And he was right.

But for one crazy moment she wished that he weren't. She wished they were different people. People who knew how to have relationships. But if time weren't the issue, it would be something else.

"Maddy and I...we love each other. We grew to depend on each other out of necessity. But...I don't think I have any more to give," he said.

She looked at him. His eyes were closed now, his body relaxing, readying for sleep. She'd fallen asleep next to Gage every night this week, listening to his deep, even breathing. And someday that would be gone. It would have to be. There was no future for them.

Pain hit her square in the chest, stole her breath.

She loved him.

She loved him, and she didn't want to. She didn't want to be in this relationship, didn't want to have to sacrifice her ambitions, didn't want to deviate from her life plans. There was no way either of them could make anything like a marriage work, not when their businesses took up all of their time.

Not when she was afraid of what it meant to be in love.

What if they grew to hate each other as much as they cared for each other now? When the misery set in, misery because they'd had to compromise too much, because Gage was tired of her, what would she be left with?

She almost laughed. She might be in love, but Gage wasn't in love with her. He'd said more than once that he didn't do serious and for him, this was just another fling, another strictly physical relationship. And now he'd outlined, in clear detail, why he wasn't meant for fatherhood or marriage.

She'd fooled herself into thinking she wanted a fling, but it had always been about more than that. She'd wanted to move past all of the issues that still hung over her head. Wanted to erase her mother's influence in her life if possible.

And instead she'd landed herself in a mess her mother would have reveled in. She loved a man who would never love her back. She loved a man she didn't want to love. She was in the relationship she'd never wanted.

She slid out of his arms and went into the living room, clutching her arms, trying to keep herself from shivering.

It didn't matter how she felt about Gage.

She laughed out loud into the empty room. It did matter. Now that she knew what her feelings meant, she knew she had to finish with him. She shook her head. She'd done what she'd promised herself, and him, she wouldn't. She'd fallen in love with her first lover.

She sank onto the couch and drew her knees up to her chest, her heart pounding so hard she thought it might break. The pain so severe she was certain it already was.

She couldn't do it. She couldn't stay. Not feeling like she did.

A tear slid down her cheek.

She was so afraid that if she stayed, she would give him everything. Everything she'd learned to hold inside, all of the emotions she'd learned to carefully suppress. And they wouldn't be enough for him, either. She wasn't enough. She never had been. Her love hadn't been enough for her own mother, why would it mean anything to him?

She pressed the heels of her hands hard against her eyes and tried to block the flow of tears. She had to be strong. She had to end it. Before he did it for her.

It was 4:00 a.m. when Gage woke up and found Lily's side of the bed cold and empty.

Lily's side of the bed.

Any other time, it would have bothered him to think of anything in his home as belonging to someone else, especially a woman he was seeing. But with Lily, it seemed natural.

He didn't feel claustrophobic when he thought of spending an indefinite amount of time with her. He wanted her, and for now that was fine. He could continue to enjoy her until the arrangement no longer benefited either of them.

He pulled on a pair of dark boxer briefs and went out into the living room. Lily was sitting there on the couch, a cup of coffee in her hand, a blank expression on her face. Her hair was pulled back into a bun and she was dressed in a fitted skirt and jacket, her work uniform.

"Did something happen with Maddy?" he asked,

thoughts of the media hounding his sister his first thought.

She shook her head, her lips pursed. "No. Maddy's fine. At least, I haven't seen anything about her in the news."

She lowered her eyes and gripped her coffee tighter. He'd spent a lot of time with Lily over the months she'd worked with him, more since they'd started sleeping together, and he knew her moods. She was upset and she was trying desperately not to show it.

His first crazy thought was that she might be pregnant, though he had been vigilant about protection. Still, a thousand images rushed through his head. Lily, her belly rounded by pregnancy. Lily, holding their baby.

The very idea should have terrified him. He'd never wanted to be a father. Not because he didn't want children, but because he didn't want to become his parents. He had the same kind of ambition both of his parents had shared, and so did Lily. They'd discussed as much only that evening. So when would they see their baby? Between work and work-related events?

But if it had already happened, there was nothing that could be done. If she was pregnant, he would face it, and he knew that she would, too. Neither of them ran from things. They faced things head-on, which was why they had more than they occasional clash.

A baby. A small surge of exhilaration rushed through him. Maybe this would be his chance. His chance to have everything he didn't believe he could ever possibly earn.

"Lily, whatever it is, you can tell me," he said, his voice tight.

"I can't do this anymore, Gage."

Her words hit him with the impact of a brick. His

stomach contracted and his chest squeezed tight. Pain ripped through him before it was washed away by a tide of anger that washed it away.

"You can't do what?" he asked, his voice soft, because he knew he was on the edge, and unless he kept himself under careful control, he might lose it completely.

"This. This relationship. Whatever it is we have. We agreed to a fling, and this—" she gestured around his home "—staying at each other's houses and going on dates and you buying my clothes, that's not a fling."

"Yes, Lily, this is a fling. It certainly isn't anything more." The pain in his chest compelled him to lash out, made him want to shatter that composed look on his face, find a break in the calm, smooth voice.

It was an incredible crash, thinking that he'd found a way to hold on to her forever, and finding out she was slipping away from him. He had nothing to hold her to him, nothing to make her want to stay.

He swallowed hard, trying to block out the incredible pain that was lashing at his heart, making him feel raw, wounded. This was why he didn't simply give emotion, didn't do caring. He had loved his parents, and it had meant nothing to them. And then, even with all of his achievements, he hadn't been enough.

He wasn't enough for Lily, either.

She looked up at him and for a moment, he was certain he saw pain in her eyes, until she masked it again with the blank expression she'd been wearing when he walked into the room.

"Then why prolong it?" she asked, standing. "I'll get a cab."

"Why? You have to be at work soon. I can drive you," he ground out.

She looked away from him. "I don't know…"

"It's just a fling, Lily," he bit out. "And we always knew that it would end. And we agreed you would continue to work for me."

She sucked in a sharp breath. "Of course. My job is important to me. Another reason why I don't think it's smart to prolong this. I don't want it affecting our work."

Something about the way she said that made his stomach burn. Her job was important. What had passed between them wasn't.

He couldn't even believe that only moments before he'd been imagining having a baby with her. Had even thought they could make it work. But she was no different than his parents, and when it came right down to it, neither was he. He might have thought, for a brief moment, that he could be someone else, that he could have another life than the one he was meant to have. But it was not possible.

"I'll get ready," he said and turned away, headed back into the bedroom and shut the door behind him. He pounded his fist hard against the wall, hoping that it might loosen some of the pain that had settled in his chest.

He shook the lingering sting from his hand and went to his closet. His chest still hurt. He wanted to back out and take her in his arms and tell her they weren't finished. He wanted to take her back to bed and pleasure her until neither of them could think. Until she didn't want to leave him.

But there was no point. This was always the way it was going to end. It was what he wanted. What he had to want. He didn't do permanent. He didn't want to be tied down for the rest of his life, to have to put himself, his job, second. He'd been there, he'd done that.

But he didn't feel a sense of freedom at the thought of ending his affair with Lily. He only felt like there was a hole inside of him. And he had no idea how he would fill it without her.

Lily sat in the chair across from Gage's desk, pen in hand, taking notes. She was gripping the pen too tightly and her hand hurt. But everything in her body hurt. To be with Gage—without being with him—was almost pure torture.

But she had agreed to it. She had agreed to the fling in the first place, and then she had instigated its demise.

But she had done it for all the right reasons. Gage had said, unequivocally, that their relationship was nothing more than a casual affair. And she had fallen in love with him.

She just needed some time away from him. Not that she was going to get any real time away from him. Not when she had to see him every day. But she wasn't about to self-destruct her career just because she'd made the stupid mistake of sleeping with her boss. And falling in love with him.

She didn't even want to be in love, so the fact that she was absolutely heartbroken over him was even worse. But what would they do in a relationship? Get married? Have a family?

It was laughable. They weren't suited to it. Neither of them wanted it.

Her heart burned in her chest. If she didn't want love, then why did the thought of having it with Gage make her ache like it did? Why did her heart feel like it was going to shatter? Why did her life, her perfect life that she had worked so hard for, suddenly feel empty?

Lily's bed felt empty. She only wished her heart could feel as empty. But it was full. Full of pain, love, need.

She rolled out of her bed and walked out onto her balcony. She could hear the waves crashing on the shore, smell the sea as the crisp wind blew over the surface of the water and carried it to her.

This was what she had worked so hard for. This view. Her home. A home that was hers alone, a life that was hers alone. One that wasn't controlled by her mother.

A tear slid down her cheek. She didn't feel free anymore. She'd imagined, for so long, that she was. Had believed that because she'd left, because she'd quit caring whether or not she was enough for her mother, that she had left it behind her.

But she hadn't. She had carried it with her. It had motivated her, made her successful in her professional life as she'd moved further and further away from her painful childhood, and made more of herself than her mother would have thought her capable of.

It had made her successful in some ways, but she had allowed it to stunt her in so many other ways. She was still letting it stop her.

She closed her eyes and breathed in deeply. She wanted Gage. She didn't know if he wanted her, not in the same way she wanted him. She didn't know if he could ever love her.

Her own mother hadn't loved her half as much as she'd loved the various men that had paraded through her life.

It galled her to find out that the thing that had kept her from a relationship, from love, was the fear that she wasn't good enough. She hid it by focusing on things she excelled at, and she simply ignored everything else, so that she didn't have to face it.

She wasn't going to do it anymore. She felt as if she was back on the edge of the cliff again, the ocean at the bottom, a swirling sea of uncertainty beneath her. She could turn and run, as she had done before, or she could face it head-on. She'd managed to do that with business, to face down opponents in the media, without breaking a sweat.

It was her personal life, her feelings, that she'd been afraid to face.

She took a deep breath, trying to lighten some of the weight that had settled in her chest. She didn't know what Gage would say if she told him she loved him. He would probably turn and run the other way. But she knew that she had to tell him. She wasn't going to live in fear anymore, not with the fear that she was unlovable, not with the fear of what might happen if she gave herself over to a relationship.

Gage had asked her once if she trusted him, and she'd said yes. But she'd lied. She hadn't trusted him. If she had, she would never have felt the need to run before he had the chance to end the relationship.

Because that was what it came down to. She was running. She'd been running since she was seventeen.

She wasn't running anymore.

Gage was at his desk at five that morning. He couldn't sleep. Not without Lily in his bed. Without her in his arms.

And she had left him. Women never left him. He was always the one to end a relationship. But not this one. Lily had left him.

He wanted her back, but if he had her, he had no idea what he would do. What he could do. Frustration roared through him. He wanted something he could never have, wanted to give Lily things he wasn't certain he knew how to give. Wanted her to feel those things in return when he knew she simply didn't.

It was not the first time it had happened to him. His parents had not wanted him, they hadn't wanted him even with all of his achievements. Why should Lily want him? He'd let her walk away because he'd always believed, deep inside of himself, that he was not a man who someone could love. And so he had set out to become a man who didn't need love. And when Lily had left, he'd told himself it was for the best.

But there was a war being waged inside of him. A war that pitted what he'd always believed about himself against his heart's newfound desire. No matter the outcome, it made him want to take a risk, to dive headlong into all of the things that Lily made him feel. Things he hadn't imagined were possible for him to feel.

He had always been the man who took care of things. When Maddy had needed him, he was there. Always. There had never been a situation in his life that he hadn't believed he could find the solution to. But there was nothing he could do now.

He wasn't the kind of man who admitted to needing. To needing help. To needing someone else. But he needed her, and there was nothing in his own power that could bring her to him, that could make her want him the way he wanted her.

He looked around his office. He had always considered this his biggest achievement, yet now, it felt like nothing. He would gladly give it up in that moment, for Lily.

He thought back on the years he'd spent raising Maddy. They had been stressful, and trying, and sometimes too much for a twenty-five-year-old man to deal with. But they had been fulfilling in a way his life hadn't been since.

There was something he could do. Something he had always vowed never to do. Not since he had told his mother he loved her when he was five and she had simply stared at him in stony silence. He could tell Lily. He could put himself on the line, his heart, his pride. What did it mean if he didn't have her?

He blew out a harsh breath and stood from his desk just as the door to his office opened. Lily stepped in, hair in a knot, prim and proper outfit skimming her curves like always. Making him want to see the beauty that lay beneath.

She turned on shut the door, the lock clicking softly.

"Gage," she said softly, her voice shaking.

He thought of the first time she'd walked into his office for a job interview. Her manner had been confident, her voice steady. She looked far removed from that woman now. There was vulnerability, real emotion.

"I didn't expect you this early," he said.

"I couldn't sleep."

"I couldn't sleep, either." Their eyes caught and held, and he knew they had both been sleepless for the same reason.

"I thought…Gage, I have to tell you," she said. "I thought that not needing anyone made me strong. I didn't want to be like my mother and need things from other people all the time. So I avoided relationships. And then I met you, and I wanted you, I wanted you enough that I thought I could take the chance and have you, and because you were only interested in temporary, you wouldn't ask anything of me."

She took a shuddering breath and continued. "But you did, Gage. You asked everything of me. You challenged me, and you asked me to do things that were hard. You wouldn't let me hide."

She reached back and pulled on the tie that was holding her hair in place and let it fall loose around her shoulders.

"I still tried to hide," she said. "I didn't want to expose myself to you. To anyone."

She unbuttoned the first button on her top, then quickly undid the rest, letting her blouse fall to the floor. Her hands shook as she undid the catch on her bra and let it fall down to the floor, too. Then she pushed her skirt down her rounded hips, leaving her standing before him in nothing more than a pair of tiny panties and some bright blue shoes.

"Image is important," she said, dragging her panties down her legs and kicking her shoes to the side. "I've always said that it was because image is a part of my job. But I was using it to hide. As long as I had all of this—" she gestured to the clothes around her feet "—I could play the part. I could pretend I was confident. Like I had everything together. But I don't. I was just afraid." She laughed. "I am afraid. But I'm not going to give you the image anymore. I'm just Lily Ford. I wasn't born with money. I worked for everything I have. And I'm afraid of being in love. Of being in love with you. Because I'm afraid that I'm not enough."

He looked at Lily, his heart hammering in his chest. Then he crossed the room and took her in his arms, her body warm and soft against him. "You're everything, Lily. Don't ever doubt it." He smoothed her silky hair, sifted his fingers through it. "I love you. When you're in your business suits ready to take on the world, and when you're crying after we've made love. I love everything about you. Every part of you. It's all you."

He felt her shoulders shake. "You love me?"

"Yes, Lily. I love you. I was as scared as you are, because I think I've loved you for a very long time, but I didn't know what to do with it. I was afraid that I wouldn't be enough for you. That I wouldn't be able to give you what you deserved. That I wouldn't be able to give our children what they deserved. I was afraid that I was like my parents, that things would always come before people. But I would give it all up today if it meant I could have you."

"I would, too," she said, her voice muffled by tears. "None of it matters if I can't share it with you."

"You don't have to give anything up for me, Lily. I love how ambitious you are. I love your wit, your humor, your drive. I would never ask you to be someone else. I want the woman you are."

"I would never ask you to change, either."

"Work isn't my life anymore," Gage said, looking at her beautiful, tearstained face. "You are. Our children will be. When you told me you were done…right before, you looked so serious, I was certain you were going to tell me you were pregnant. And I was scared, because I didn't know if I could be a good father. I didn't know if I could love a child properly, not after how I was raised. I didn't know if that child could love me. But I knew if I was going to have a child, I wanted it to be with you."

"Gage…" She put her hand on his cheek. "Our children will love you. And I love you. I can't help myself. Our parents were screwed up, but we don't have to be."

"No, we don't."

"Of course, you know that if we get married, I'll have access to all of your dirty laundry, and my job will only be more difficult, since I'm going to have to hide all of your flaws from the public, when I'm aware of every single one of them."

He laughed and smoothed his hands down her back, over her bare curves. "You love my flaws."

She whimpered. "I do. And you love mine."

"More than I love my own."

"We can do this, Gage," she said, her voice trembling. "We can have this."

"Of course we can, Lily. Love isn't what your mother had, love isn't what my parents gave to my sister and me. This is love. What I feel for you. All of the things I'd worked for suddenly meant nothing without you to share them with."

"That's exactly how I felt. Everything that I was happy with before was empty if you weren't there. I always liked empty before I met you, Gage, but now it just feels hollow."

"Lily, I think we need to sign another contract."

"Really?"

"I do. One that says we're going to stay together, for better or for worse, for all of our lives."

"I would definitely sign that," she said, smiling through her tears.

"Was that an agreement?"

She kissed him, long and hard, with all of the passion and love they felt coursing between them. "Yes, it was. But I'm not thinking a handshake is how I want to seal the deal."

"Oh, no," he said. "I can think of so many better ways to celebrate this union."

"Show me," she whispered against his lips.

"For the rest of our lives."

* * * * *

Coming Next Month

from **Harlequin Presents® EXTRA.** Available September 13, 2011.

Coming Next Month

from **Harlequin Presents®.** Available September 27, 2011.

REQUEST YOUR FREE BOOKS!

Harlequin *Presents*

PASSION GUARANTEED SEDUCTION

2 FREE NOVELS PLUS
2 FREE GIFTS!

YES! Please send me 2 FREE Harlequin Presents® novels and my 2 FREE gifts (gifts are worth about $10). After receiving them, if I don't wish to receive any more books, I can return the shipping statement marked "cancel." If I don't cancel, I will receive 6 brand-new novels every month and be billed just $4.30 per book in the U.S. or $4.99 per book in Canada. That's a saving of at least 14% off the cover price! It's quite a bargain! Shipping and handling is just 50¢ per book in the U.S. and 75¢ per book in Canada.* I understand that accepting the 2 free books and gifts places me under no obligation to buy anything. I can always return a shipment and cancel at any time. Even if I never buy another book, the two free books and gifts are mine to keep forever.

106/306 HDN FERQ

Name	(PLEASE PRINT)	

Address		Apt. #

City	State/Prov.	Zip/Postal Code

Signature (if under 18, a parent or guardian must sign)

Mail to the **Reader Service:**
IN U.S.A.: P.O. Box 1867, Buffalo, NY 14240-1867
IN CANADA: P.O. Box 609, Fort Erie, Ontario L2A 5X3

Not valid for current subscribers to Harlequin Presents books.

**Are you a current subscriber to Harlequin Presents books
and want to receive the larger-print edition?
Call 1-800-873-8635 or visit www.ReaderService.com.**

* Terms and prices subject to change without notice. Prices do not include applicable taxes. Sales tax applicable in N.Y. Canadian residents will be charged applicable taxes. Offer not valid in Quebec. This offer is limited to one order per household. All orders subject to credit approval. Credit or debit balances in a customer's account(s) may be offset by any other outstanding balance owed by or to the customer. Please allow 4 to 6 weeks for delivery. Offer available while quantities last.

Your Privacy—The Reader Service is committed to protecting your privacy. Our Privacy Policy is available online at www.ReaderService.com or upon request from the Reader Service.

We make a portion of our mailing list available to reputable third parties that offer products we believe may interest you. If you prefer that we not exchange your name with third parties, or if you wish to clarify or modify your communication preferences, please visit us at www.ReaderService.com/consumerschoice or write to us at Reader Service Preference Service, P.O. Box 9062, Buffalo, NY 14269. Include your complete name and address.

HP11B

*Harlequin Romantic Suspense presents the latest book
in the scorching new* KELLEY LEGACY *miniseries
from best-loved veteran series author Carla Cassidy*

*Scandal is the name of the game as the Kelley family fights
to preserve their legacy, their hearts…and their lives.*

Read on for an excerpt from the fourth title
RANCHER UNDER COVER

*Available October 2011
from Harlequin Romantic Suspense*

"Would you like a drink?" Caitlin asked as she walked to the minibar in the corner of the room. She felt as if she needed to chug a beer or two for courage.

"No, thanks. I'm not much of a drinking man," he replied.

She raised an eyebrow and looked at him curiously as she poured herself a glass of wine. "A ranch hand who doesn't enjoy a drink? I think maybe that's a first."

He smiled easily. "There was a six-month period in my life when I drank too much. I pulled myself out of the bottom of a bottle a little over seven years ago and I've never looked back."

"That's admirable, to know you have a problem and then fix it."

Those broad shoulders of his moved up and down in an easy shrug. "I don't know how admirable it was, all I knew at the time was that I had a choice to make between living and dying and I decided living was definitely more appealing."

She wanted to ask him what had happened preceding that six-month period that had plunged him into the bottom of the bottle, but she didn't want to know too much about him. Personal information might produce a false sense of intimacy that she didn't need, didn't want in her life.

"Please, sit down," she said, and gestured him to the table. She had never felt so on edge, so awkward in her life.

"After you," he replied.

She was aware of his gaze intensely focused on her as she rounded the table and sat in the chair, and she wanted to tell him to stop looking at her as if she were a delectable dessert he intended to savor later.

Watch Caitlin and Rhett's sensual saga unfold amidst the shocking, ripped-from-the-headlines drama of the Kelley Legacy miniseries in

RANCHER UNDER COVER

Available October 2011 only from Harlequin Romantic Suspense, wherever books are sold.

HRSEXP1011

USA TODAY bestselling author

Carol Marinelli

brings you her new romance

HEART OF THE DESERT

One searing kiss is all it takes for Georgie to know
Sheikh Prince Ibrahim is trouble....

But, trapped in the swirling sands, Georgie finally
surrenders to the brooding rebel prince—yet the
law of his land decrees that she can never
really be his....

Available October 2011.

Available only from Harlequin Presents®.

Harlequin®

SPECIAL EDITION

Life, Love and Family

Look for
NEW YORK TIMES AND *USA TODAY*
BESTSELLING AUTHOR

KATHLEEN EAGLE

in October!

Recently released and wounded war vet
Cal Cougar is determined to start his recovery—
inside and out. There's no better place than the
Double D Ranch to begin the journey.
Cal discovers firsthand how extraordinary the
ranch really is when he meets a struggling single
mom and her very special child.

ONE BRAVE COWBOY,
available September 27 wherever books are sold!

www.Harlequin.com

SE656257KE